SLICED AMERICANA

SLICED
AMERICANA

JIM WATKINS

Sharon Green, Tom Riedel

Is It Wet Yet Press

I

Arise a Hero

Chuck, Percy, and I were drinking at the bar Saturday. We were just talking shit when Chuck pointed out Brad, who was a guy he went to high school with.

"Oh my God!" He squealed, "That's my friend Brad!"

"Go say hi, Chuck, ask him if he wants to join us." Percy persuaded.

"Oh, I couldn't. I doubt he would remember me." He gasped.

"If you don't think he would remember you, then I would hardly consider him a friend, Chuck," I added sarcastically.

That's where it began. We argued, discussed, and came up with our drunken yet genius theory.

Everyone you know fits into a certain category. The categories were decidedly dubbed as follows: family, friends, acquaintances, and everyone else. Obviously, everyone knows who the first three are. Who is everyone else?

That took some careful consideration, much discussion, and more than a few beers before a unanimous agreement was reached. Everyone else was inside three sub-categories.

1. The checker at the gas station who sells you lottery tickets twice a week is a "thrust-upon."
2. The people you see all the time. Like, say, at the bus stop across the street from yours. These are people you never speak to but are "recognizable."
3. Finally, all the people you used to know. Whose names you don't remember, and who probably wouldn't remember yours. They are "gone, but not completely forgotten."

(Brad fit into this slot)

I thought the whole theory was quite clever, and a little amusing. Eventually, I sobered up. It's pretty safe to say that alcohol can inspire some creative subjects and odd conclusions. Like the ones I experience in my weekly therapy sessions, minus the beer.

Therapy is more than likely useless. You are what you are. What I should want out of therapy, is to want to stop loving it. I need to be cured of pain by paying someone a hundred and sixty dollars an hour to listen to my bullshit. I can't blame the doctor for not fixing my problem; my addiction is her paycheck. The situation is an oxymoron in more ways than one.

My love of therapy began when I was in grade school. My folks thought my behavior was a bit questionable and decided I needed a psychological evaluation. I surely did. My sister needed the same but hid it better. The truth about my homelife was never revealed to the therapist. I wouldn't dare. I learned to enjoy therapy, so I had to make up ridiculous and damning lies to secure a permanent place on the couch.

Eventually, my parents were investigated by Child Protective Services. They were investigating the wrong people, so they never found any wrongdoing. I was declared a chronic liar and continued my treatment. It gave me a thrill. Now I had something to look forward to. Thursdays between three and four every week, I would be in my happy place. Nowadays I have plenty of fucked up true stories to tell the good doctor. All of them thanks to my family, friends, acquaintances, and those people that are gone, but not completely forgotten.

The first thing I noticed when I walked in the room was

the window. It was directly across from the unusually tall, worn, dingy wooden door, with an incredibly loose antique glass knob. It hosted old vertical blinds covered in dust and fly crap. It was surprising how much light passed through the blinds. Considering their neglected condition. They were sporting a hefty crack from top to bottom and thirty years of nicotine on the inside. With an equally aged amount of bird shit on the outside. Underneath the stream of heavily filtered sunlight that highlighted about a billion dust particles sat a couch. It was worn leather, the color of an old copper penny. I imagined the number of crazy asses that contributed to the two equal depressions on each of the button-covered cushions. Directly in the middle of the room sat an old bulky desk. It was covered in the shit that desks keep off the floor. Stapler, papers, framed photos of ugly children, and a stained novelty coffee cup, reading I "heart" my shrink. Hanging heavily over the desk was a ceiling fan. The fan was larger than a room of this size needed. Smothered with dust, I had to look twice to be sure it wasn't actually covered in faux fur.

Butted up against the ancient scarred desk was a woman. She sat in a tall chair speaking on a cell phone. I let out a phony cough designed to alert the unaware. It worked. She gestured me over to the crusty couch without even glancing in my direction. I made my way to the nearest ass divot and eased myself down. Surprisingly it was comfortable. She snapped her flip-phone shut and gave me a huge welcoming smile. She must have been thinking about the check I would be writing on my way out. I realized right then that I hated doctors. I also hated the fact that I couldn't stand the thought of not having one. She asked me how I was doing today; original line, must be a Harvard gal.

I returned with a brilliant "fine." This was my first visit to Dr. Kelley.

My previous shrink was Dr. Lewis. He recently retired. Currently, he's spending the money he acquired from me over the past several years. I would imagine he is enjoying a pretty solid retirement.

Starting with a new therapist meant starting over from the bitter beginning. Would I have the strength? She sat there, her head slightly tilted to one side, hands folded neatly on her lap. I began with a short loud clearing of my throat and a few nervous body adjustments. My whole sordid story began to slip out from between my lips. From chronic lying as a child to stay in therapy, to actually needing it as an adult. I was hearing myself telling my story fresh to someone new. It made me realize my addiction to therapy was the enjoyment of the attention I received. Going back and forth with my reasoning and rationalizations made me realize I may never actually know why I keep coming. As long as I'm here, then I will make her earn every penny of the large check that will soon be written.

Dr. Kelley spoke. "Please tell me about your friends and relationships."

**

When writing a story, some thought is necessary to plan a plot. No amount of trying will keep a storyline straight without a plan to follow. Keeping in line and following that set plan will weld a story for most folks to follow. Simple, boring, easy to guess the next phrase, thought, or concept satisfies most. The story is not unique. Its purpose is to fill a void. Filling in time with a wall of words that follow the same formula that many before and all too many after will as well. Accumulation of adjectives, adverbs, and auxiliaries hold together story paths. The same set path the typical Friday evening read develops - developing in comfort without sharp confusing edges that have a possibility of cutting. The plot carefully digs into preconceived beliefs. Feeling safe and normal, thus avoiding offending the common man.

Let's keep the story focused. Pointing in the right direction along an unbreakable storyline is imperative. This keeps the entertainment value consistent. Publishers want the satisfaction proven results return. With proven results, there's no chance, no possible way to confuse the motive. Thus providing certain profit to the publishing house.

We are all willing victims. Staying in our zone of comfort without the fear of changing our perceptions. The view of reality fixed in our minds being the most important pillar of our structured reality. Bending a braced abutment out of place with purposeful destructive intent might twist a common unmemorable proven plot into a messy pile of construction material, the hot mess of uncompleted work. To be set on fire without another thought. Whereby removing the offensive thoughts from view. Nobody's hurt. Everyone loses when individual uniqueness no longer separates the ordinary from the special.

Let's break the formula a bit by adding in a new concept. It may require a warning label. If we put a cellophane wrapper on the book, the purity of housewives across the nation will persevere. Nobody needs to take responsibility for exposing them to new dangerous ideas. Hardworking men don't want to come home and find their wives exposed to new thoughts and theories.

"Dinner on the table yet, Darling? Where's my beer? That's a good girl. Let's watch some TV, then go to bed. Tomorrow will come soon, and Sunday is still a long way off."

It's happening all over. We all conform to the media's ideal. What should we do with our time? Most find it acceptable to pad their thoughts with facts that support an existing belief. Making room in a busy life for unique new ideas may prove upsetting. It's best to seek out soothing material supportive of our thoughts. Which builds our confirmation-bias stronger, strengthening our will.

We don't need this stimulation to exist. Our needs are simple. Our desires have little to do with what keeps the body alive. We need to sleep, eat and work. When there's an opportunity to procreate, welcome the moment. This keeps our common soul pointed at the target. We continue moving down the path towards inevitability and nameless obscurity.

When a new thought or concept comes along. Accepting it depends on its introduction. New concepts need gentle introductions. Men need to follow a well-worn path, slowly exposing them and increasing their social consciousness. Gradually learning new concepts is comfortable. The common man will follow along when the story's path is comfortable with his expectation of reality.

Working people are doing something. Their value to the economy is immense, even without a formal advanced education. The working class has the ability to connect motive with deed, bringing focus on the intent behind typical propaganda.

The average man on the street making his way to work knows and can see through most propaganda and lies. He may not be able to put his finger on who is attempting social manipulation. There may be confusion on what is being manipulated. Yet, there is no doubt inside his mind when the manipulation is going on. He can feel and will know something is not right in the social scene he is part of.

Effective stories are based on truths. Even the most fantastical of fantasies needs grounding if you want the public to buy the plot. Buy is the keyword. Someone with a few bills in their wallet needs to pull them out and lay them down on the counter. Otherwise, your story will never amount to anything.

There is no need to write to the permanently unemployable. These folks are the manipulated mass. There is power in their numbers, but buying power is not it. Permanently unemployed are easily entertained with a simple melody, sports, and violence. The larger government groups control their massive buying power. The normal author trying to sell a nice story will rarely have the power to break into this market. The state controls their wealth, which they see as an all-powerful entity providing daily sustenance.

The wealth of the masses is created by the worker. The wealthiest in our society control this capital. They collect the tax from working men. Minions distribute it to the unemployable while skimming a spiff off the top. There is a real genius in the ability to keep this engine of iniquity spinning. Teaching the unemployable to support themselves is not in the plan.

Reality is an intimate relationship. Putting carbohydrates

in the belly and having a place to stay is all most people care about. They won't take a chance that may result in the potential loss of those things. Only folks that have lost; or are willing to lose them will rise up.

The media drones on, making much out of the inconsequential. Hiding the important lurid reality from naive consumers, as life goes on. The people have become disenfranchised by the powerful that govern them.

There are those that search with a yearning need for a hero. Their champion is someone to rally behind, returning the country to the way things were, thoughts of a kinder time. When being in control of your own destiny are thoughts that shouldn't be spoken. These secret thoughts of liberty and freedom are shut up inside heads by people that no longer have the words to express their thoughts.

The existence of a belief and hope for a better future will bring scorn in the mild case to an individual. In severe circumstances, others become infected with their optimistic thoughts. This can result in permanent separation from their community. Retraining and relocation are certain outcomes. Extreme cases of independent thought bring the ultimate penalty. Tremble, considering your words and actions before allowing your opinions and thoughts to become public. Know that punishment is incoming whenever you cross the State's official talking points.

The benefit and accolades received for extolling an approved viewpoint are minimal when it's compared to the severity of punishment for unapproved thinking. Silence is the best course to set. Listening and analyzing the news received. Form your opinions in silence. Wait for that hero to arise, someone to free everybody from the enslavement of modern post-industrialized society.

2

Zephir

SENATVS CONSVLTVM VLTIMVM

Use any means necessary to defend the Republic.

Each generation has a right to redefine a role and must, according to their time. ~ Diana Rigg
The thirteen virtues of Benjamin Franklin
Temperance Sincerity
Silence Justice
Order Moderation
Resolution Cleanliness
Frugality Tranquility
Industry Chastity
and
Humility

Zephir always gently from the sea breathes on them, to refresh the happy race. ~ Homer

God save our immortal souls. Define that which is good as the bar you need to jump over. The powerful will be forgiving only of power. Ceaselessly praying for the hunger to subside. We will then find rest and be able to abide.

The crooked way is rapid and effective, but life is long and our souls are immortal.

When an object travels near the speed of light and is viewed with a narrow angle from a distance, it will appear to be moving at more than the speed of light. This is called superluminal velocity. It represents a frame of reference to time and location - an illusion, which of course it is not. Locally, the object appears to be at a speed below that of photons.

The measurement of consciousness must cause the collapse of the wave function. At the minuscule levels of microtubules, the observation of the wave function inside of the noise that is the brain in a conscious state causes a collapse. This happens every time a measurement of consciousness is attempted. Our observations of the quantum that is inside the waking mind of all creatures. Of course at what level a living animal is conscious enough to have a sentient mind may not have an impact on a wave.

Is an insect sentient?

Perhaps not, but is it conscious?

When an ant observes a measurement of an electron will its observation be relevant to the experiment?

It is doubtful that an ants observation would effect the wave function, but would a cat's observation have an effect, or cause the collapse of the wave function?

These are serious questions. Our current machines with AI may have the intellect of a rat. Would a rat's observation cause decoherence? Would the AI's mechanical sentience cause the collapse under the conditions as a man?

The arrow of time is only one way in 4D spacetime. The brilliant theoretical physics professors know this, but the common man struggles to understand, even in the figures, pictures, etc they use to explain time and space to humanity. They leave out what they know to be true, but struggle to explain. The math explains it clearly. No quaint description will. Most people never learn enough to understand that time has at least three dimensions like material matter. That which we can see or touch also has at least three. Where there are three dimensions there must be four. Those three dimensions of space require a fourth spacial dimension to enclose the spacial dimensions thus the three dimensions of time also require a fourth dimension of time to enclose our spacetime.

There are more dimensions. Current String Theory uses 11. There are at least eight we can build models of. There must be to justify Inflation theory. To show the multiple eons or epochs that are predicted by Sir Roger Penrose and Steven Hawking.

Sir Roger would argue we have just the 4 and they are all wrapped up in a game of Twister Theory. Let's not argue about it. There will be mistakes and genius epiphanies along the way to our final destination. Garret Lisi has shown us what the shadow of particles from the eighth dimension was on us in the third dimension. The E8 shines its shadow down to the third dimension due to this maverick physicist's brilliant work. The model he gave us leaves a fantastical view of what we may only see in its shadow form.

Consciousness must be something other than this. We

can't have our conscious thoughts collapsing every time they are observed. It has to be something else. There must be more to it than the simple explanation we receive, or nonexplanation that we don't receive.

Let's observe local action and interaction among natives. I bring you to a village on planet Earth. Thanking continually those higher dimensional beings referred to as angels for helping me make the right turns. We all have plenty of opportunity. We have the ability to move in many directions. Each direction of movement is equally valid. Each doorway opened by turning left instead of right or standing fast instead of moving is a new reality. Don't forget to thank those creatures that help us from dimensions beyond those that we consciously experience. We exist in all reality. Experiencing the brilliance of more than one now simultaneously is more than our minds have the capability to comprehend. Don't give in or relent when there is a chance of success and right is on your side. Be inspired by the happiness we pursue. There are infinite possibilities as we follow the arrow of time. Whether that arrow is bent, straight, or forked like Poseidon's trident.

The squeezed atoms of entire star systems are manipulating space-time into jolly glowing giant black holes. The goo of these many squeezed worlds forging elements that have Neve been seen before. The gigantic Sagittarius A at the center of our galaxy is eating and squeezing more mass with a fantastic variety of elements. Good eating, and creating the actual elements and shiny new elements that become by the squeeze.

Society's norms have changed for a long while. In fact, they are constantly changing, as we swim in the tide of time. Fads come and go and we as society adjust to them. There is no telling for taste. Whether it's a heaping helping of cottonseed oil in your pancakes, or perhaps you prefer a little olive oil. Whichever you consider better may depend on your position in multi-universal-time-space. Your heart and mind can decide what you take a bite out of. That decision will put you down the path of a new future. We are constantly making these decisions.

For sure, know that nobody is innocent of dipping into decadent thoughts or daydreaming about depraved thoughts. Considering murder doesn't make you a murderer. Making a list of people that would be better off to have never existed and imagining those folks dead, doesn't either. Surprisingly, many people have such lists.

It is soothing to consider making the world a better place. That place of tranquility. The place where people get along and there is no strife; that place with no arguments only exists inside of your mind. Even inside your head, there is a constant argument going on between good, or evil, right and wrong. How can it be otherwise?

The list you made was wrong. It is not okay to erase the future presence of Darren from the Universe because he stole your lunchbox in 6th grade. Even though, he found himself on your list of better off dead individuals. The thought of Darren dead at the time made you feel better, and he did exist for a time in that state of dead, not dead. He was in a superposition between the two states until you made the decision to not kill Darren for his theft. This was probably the correct decision to make. Time will weigh in on Darren, and the lunchbox incident will be forgotten. The future will be there splitting before us. Constantly, and smoothly opening up our realities to the next here and now where we always abide.

Our future does split. It is constantly peeling off on new paths. From our position which is the vertex of the event. We travel only one ray consciously, we create it by our actions. Yet according to quantum mechanics, the universe is pixelated. So we must hop from vertex to vertex. If you stood at the hypotenuse and looked back towards the vertex. It would all be visible.

Now of course we don't live on a simple 2d plane. We are actively in a 4d space-time interacting consciously with a 5d world that includes a dimension of electromagnetism. Coxeter discusses this and on a localized level these polygons that double back on themselves are called holosnubs. The story must go on, and understanding past the rudimentary level is not necessary to enjoy it. Let's have fun and call them hyper-pyramids.

The vertex of our triangle is our home in space-time. Now, that triangle is of course a pyramid. Think of a pyramid with more than three dimensions. That hyper-pyramid of "n" dimensions is our big physical world. This hyper-solid has been mathematically proven to the 8th dimension where it received the exciting name E8 by Garret Lisi the Nobel Prize winning surfer from Hawaii. Let's just call it a hyper-pyramid because that sounds more fun than E8. Hang Ten, Dr. Lisi, and thank you for your extraordinary work.

Our position at the vertex of the hyper-pyramid is the ultimate position of choice. Everything happens based on choice. Turning left instead of right, the ray of the next nth dimension of the hyper-pyramid emerges. If we turn right, then that ray of the hyper-pyramid of our existence unfolds in front of us. Of course, the left ray is there too. It is an equally valid path, but your personal consciousness is not on it.

Humans are unable to experience the full effect of reality. The full effect of our existence is however experienced by the rest of the Universe. Our brain, as sophisticated as we feel it is, does not see the multiple paths. It only sees one, or another. This is a binary limitation of our structure. It is how we see the world in a binary choice. We go left, we go right, we go up, we go down. We decide to do or not to do. Etc ad naseum and on and on forever.

It is possible therefore that as our unconscious souls move down those rays towards the next vertex of our personal universe's hyper-pyramid that we could double back. Hyper shapes have that wonderful capability. They are not the simple shapes we have seen since pre-school. They are the shape of our past and future. The triangle and pyramid may not be that shape, but surely it is one of the three basic polytopes that exist in higher dimensions being spun out at unimaginable angles. There will be times and places they double back and meet. It must be so, since our unlikely cast of American wretched refuse is about to meet at the same vertex, on the same timeline, in the same universe of the multi-verse our God has so graciously given us.

3

American Mujahideen

The enemy of my enemy is my friend ~ Gabriel Manigault

Will we be turned into mujahideen in our own country? Sooner or later, and it is likely sooner, you will be in a position where you have to choose. The government is not backing down. As the face of tyranny stares in your face smirking, you will have to choose at that moment - whether that time is the time you must make a stand. There is a choice to walk away. Avoiding risk is the logical choice. The smart move is to let the trouble pass you and live to an old age, free from the worry and trouble standing up and defending liberty may be.

Do you want to know who changed America? Digging in and standing for something, Dr. Martin Luther King JR did. He was the voice behind the movement. Civil rights have been written in stone because of his words. America became a shining example of freedom. Civil rights happened. In spite of constant efforts to keep the status quo, the deep state of things is unhinged when entire populations become united as one force. Be neighbors who understand each other's differences. Politically, spiritually and intimately we are all more alike than different. Our culture is for the most part seared into our souls from a young age. Let there be no doubt that the evil-hearted among us have learned these truths too.

Time for these evildoers is a straight arrow. The arrow of time points off to forever. For some, that forever is a longing to be in a place of eternal happiness. Some see it as a blackness of absolute zero and nothingness. There are thoughts and religions that see an eternal roundhouse. The place we merely spin about like the engine of a train. Death bringing yet another track to follow. Yet another load to deliver along the eternal journey we all follow. Each death and birth locking us into place in a universal caste system, with each of us just another cog in the works of an eternal spiritual engine.

These beliefs ingrained in us by our mentors and peers are difficult to rise above and change. When you have learned from a young age and experienced the festivals. Where participating in the prayers, offerings and dedications built the perspective that your view of the world is based upon.

When you face adversity and place a banana in front of Ganesha, asking for your path to be cleared. This is your upbringing. For the most part, this will always be your spiritual view of the world. Over time, the rituals and sacrifices will evolve. Melding into something new, but serving the same purpose.

There was a time in Ancient Europe and Western Asia that the gods, whether they be Athena, or Elohim of the Jews were offered the fat and organs of sheep. Appropriate festivals and ceremonies were prescribed to ensure the proper spiritual piety and necessity of the offerings made to God.

In the modern era, we see less of the lamb offerings to a pantheon of gods and goddesses in the West because of a strong belief among the majority that the Christ being the son of God, became the lamb. Who was sacrificed to his Father. The God of Moses, Isaac, Abraham, all the way back to Adam. Who was the first man.

This particular culture is the culture modern Europe was founded on. There came a cultural retrenchment. After this metamorphosis, the foundations of Puritan Christian principles were no longer accepted in Europe society. European Christianity had already evolved into modern Christian secular religious beliefs - those that wished to stick to the old ways. Those with other heretical beliefs took to the sea. These pilgrims crossed the Atlantic to settle the North American continent.

Certainly there was intense perseverance in order for these colonies of Christian men and women to survive. Some failed miserably, suffering on to the death of every single soul belonging to their particular expeditions.

The last portion of the Fifteenth century when Christopher Columbus secured funding for the most memorable adventure. It was an adventure which we all are aware of. Queen Isabella would be the facilitator of Columbus's success, even though she didn't know of his actual failure to find the short-cut to India. Her success was in investing for the future in her soon to become Empire's ability to trade.

Make no mistake this was both an economic and religious conquest. Spain had only recent been taken from the Moors. Islamic culture failed and Roman Catholicism would spread across the ocean by the Spanish Inquisition, who took it to the extreme. Annihilation lay in the path of any other belief system of these spiritual warriors of God.

The Sixteenth century was boldly led around the world by the Spanish. It was unstoppable. The momentum built up and the winds of Destiny pushed them further to the West, until they faced the East from a Western view and took a step to far.

The Spanish expeditions sent further west were able to gain one more pearl out of the Pacific. Their final big success came in conquering the Philippine Islands. Where the Mexican invaders, outnumbered by the mostly Muslim and Hindu native populations, established their final big success as an empire.

There was an attempt made to take and hold more ground. Furthering the boundaries of the Spanish empire that had started to expand over a century prior. The Spaniards decided to push into the Asian continent. Who knows what they were thinking. Likely they were complacent, arrogant and full of hubris. After all, completing the task of expanding Isabella's empire to the Indies would bring spectacular wealth. It might have cemented Spain's position as a world leader permanently, even into these days we live in.

We learn from our history and know that the English defeated the Spanish Armada in 1588. Sir Francis Drake and the rest of the English were able to soundly end Spain's aspirations of conquering England. We don't learn about the other end of the Spanish empire being cut off by the Cambodians.

Spain's last great attempt at colonization was an attempt to occupy Cambodia. This would be the last major attempt by the Spanish. It turns out that mainland Asia, and the Cambodians in particular were a lot tougher than the Spanish anticipated. Spain had expected an easy victory over island aborigines and tiny kingdoms like those that inhabited the Philippine Islands. It turns out that wasn't the case when they made this inglorious attempt of pillaging the continent of Asia. The history of this is not hidden. It is written about fairly and honestly by the Spanish Inquisition and is published in Mexico City.

If those Spaniards had established a significant foothold on mainland Asia. Our entire history would have been written in Spanish. There would be significant mention of the Christianization and colonization of Asia by the Inquisition.

The English Protestants and later the Mormons had significant influence over the shaping of America and the rest of the world. If it hadn't been for the valiant defense of their homeland by the Cambodian's that may never have happened. Most Americans don't realize how close they became to being Spaniards. This is the path our version of America lays across.

**

I was halfway down the stairwell to my less than desirable basement apartment, when I noticed an unusually large mass looming at the bottom. It was dark, so I stopped to get a better look before proceeding. My first thought was that someone's walrus was on the loose. I stood with my eyes squinted, but it wasn't until I heard a meow that I realized it was a cat. I decided to finish my descent; I could tell he was watching me as I slowly moved towards him. He was sitting on the storm drain next to my front door. Surely he would make a break for it when I came to close, but he didn't. I found myself standing right in front of him. He was waiting for me to let him inside. I put my key in the lock. As soon as the door clicked open a crack. He used his huge cross-eyed face to push his way through to the interior of my apartment. I followed him in. This was the biggest cat I had ever seen, one of those brown siamese ones, sniffing everything in his path. I stood watching him inspect every inch of the place. I kept a close eye on him. Marking this new territory would not be allowed. The fuzzy dice following closely behind him let me know he was a male.

He made his way to the large L shaped couch left over from the 70s. It was covered in a stained fabric of green and brown plaid. Surprisingly, his leap was refined as he jumped on the side arm of the couch. His hefty mass moving gracefully through the air. He proceeded to make himself comfortable. Folding his legs under his chest, lowering his butt, then wrapping his tail around his practically his entire girth. He was there, looking like a huge overcooked Thanksgiving turkey. That big turkey that could possibly feed a family gathering of thirty. I assumed he needed a place to stay, and figured he would be a pretty good roommate. I knew right off that he wouldn't pay his share of the rent. That was something you usually found out later.

I went to K-mart and bought a litter box, scoop-able sand, cat food and a few other accessories. The litter shovel and a six-pack of pink and blue furry mice looked nice. My bowls were already of pet quality. I used what was in the cupboard for his food and water. He eats out of the Tony the Tiger bowl I ordered off of a cereal box many moons ago. I named him Boyd, and immediately scheduled his altering for the following Friday.

Boyd is now my best bud. He has his faults, but what are a few scratches on the furniture, and an occasional puke pile, compared to his unconditional love? I find few of my other friends measure up to him. Some come close; most of them use the toilet, and only a handful have barfed on my carpet. If I had to choose a second best to Boyd, it would be Chuck.

I sat down to watch my 70-inc LCD Christmas present which is mounted on the wall directly across from my personal ass-niche on the L-shaped couch. Every Monday evening on channel 66 they have a marathon of "Oldies but Goldies." Eight hours of complete nostalgic bliss fragmented into thirty-minute increments of pure, unadulterated entertainment make Monday TV night. It's also Chuck night.

Just after 7 pm, ten minutes into F-Troop, the door cracks open a touch, and a whiff of Armani floats into the room. Chuck's low but amazingly feminine voice chimes his usual greeting. He pushes himself the rest of the way into the apartment, grocery store bag filled with the evening's salty snacks in the left hand, six-pack of Diet Coke in the right. Groceries go on the coffee table before he heads for the linen closet and pulls out a pink and yellow floral bed sheet. Chuck's a little apprehensive of the "big L": he finds it to be a bit on the repugnant side. The sheet serves as a buffer between him and the pestilence embedded in the ancient fabric. Once the couch condom is in place, he makes himself comfortable He won't move for the next two hours and three Diet Cokes. He takes a seven-minute piss, and returns and repeats. This scenario is exactly the same every week, without fail.

Our evenings are quiet. We focus on the superb line-up. An occasional smart-ass remark is common, especially during the commercials. I watch Chuck licking cheese dust off of his fingers, then take a huge swig of room temperature Diet Coke. I don't know why he won't keep it in the fridge. He lets out nauseating guttural burps and attempts to mute them with a puffy, pallid, and oversized ladylike hand. It's always the same comment afterwards. "Did you hear it?"

4

Happy New Years

I remember a fateful night that we shared several years ago. I was half-drunk and ready to go much earlier than nine o'clock when I was scheduled to meet Chuck at his place. Boyd was asleep in my spot on the couch, so with no place to sit, I went upstates a half an hour before he expected me. Chuck lives in the shithole apartment directly above mine. When I knocked on his door, he yelled for me to come in.

The first thing you notice about Chuck's eight hundred dollars a month mold garden of a flat is the feminine touches. There's always a large vase of cheap grocery store flowers on his coffee table. Then there are the fresh vacuum tracks in the dated carpet scented with Glade "spring rain." The air freshener mixes with the ever-present essence of mildew in the air. The smell is not of putrefaction; it's just annoying. After a moment, the odor disappears into the background. It hangs around in my presence, but my nose stops noticing it. He poked his head out of the bathroom to coo how early I was and to make myself comfortable.

It's easy to feel right at home in Chuck's place. He has done so much with so little. Our apartments are anatomically identical, but our decorating styles differ significantly. Chuck's place is as clean as a dump can be and festooned ala inexpensive sheik.

Mine could be described as clad in vintage rummage sale, with a touch of cat hair. It is safe to sit on his couch in black pants and not worry about where the lint roller is and if there is fresh tape on it. He tries to convey a sense of elegance in all his rooms, not easy on a limited budget, but he does his best to surprise. I notice an attempt in the form of a decanter full of brandy on a silver tray. There was a group of little glasses sitting around it. I filled one up. Taking a sip, I realized it tasted like gasoline smells, but I hated to let the perfectly delightful buzz I brought with me fade away into the evening.

I drank. I snooped, and I started to get bored. It's after nine, and I'm not early anymore. I decided to make my way around the end table and past the economical yet stylish dining room set to the bathroom overstuffed with all the homosexual glory that is Chuck. I bounced off of the doorframe before poking my head in. I slurred a bit as I asked him if we would be going out some time tonight? He slammed his eyeliner pencil into the sink and spun around to face me. Holy shit. I had known Chuck for a long time, but I had never seen him like this before. My drunken exaggerated expression more than likely told him what I was thinking. He had glitter on his eyebrows, false eyelashes, and a flagrant blond wig that somehow piled into a bouffant monstrosity. I wasn't sure how he stuffed himself into that tiny leather skirt or the sequined tank. My God, he had fit stilettos onto his men's size 13 feet. Where did he find size 13 stilettos?!

He just stood there. Daring me with his eyes to comment. Instead of accepting his challenge, I backed up and shut the door: I didn't think getting my ass kicked by a six-foot drag queen would be the way to start my evening.

We had decided weeks ago to attend the party at Cool-Jay's for New Year's Eve. They were hosting a fifty-dollar per person "all you can eat." Which included appetizers, well drinks, and cheap beer. It would be a real celebration, literally a "who's who" of the gay community, and a lip-sync drag show at midnight. It was also within walking or staggering distance. What more could we ask for?

We walked in through the bright red seven hundred pound front door adorned with one of the tackiest plastic Santa welcome plaques ever manufactured. Chuck loved it. He said. "We should nab it on the way out. This place is crazy!"

We finally got out and arrived at 10:30 PM. It seemed everyone else had started to party around noon. I understood that Cool-Jay's was a gay bar, but I wasn't aware that 'gay' took on a whole new meaning on New Year's Eve. This was to be my first experience waiting for the ball to drop amongst Chuck and all the other girls.

I doubt we were even three feet in the door before I was grabbed by the waist of my jeans and lifted off the floor, flopping forward and feeling my hands slap the dirty cement in front of my shoes. It wasn't a good start. I learned later that Carl had a bad habit of introducing himself by flexing his muscles.

His laugh was hardy a huge guffaw but with a slightly sinister undertone. It startled me, but Chuck moved in and gave Carl an enthusiastic hello and a broad smile. They hugged, and Chuck left a kiss-shaped lipstick mark on his cheek. Obviously, they knew each other. Their laughter made me feel a bit more at ease. My guard remained up. The evening was turning into a big gay dodging fest for me, but Chuck made himself a target, and a hell of a target he was. My estimate of over three hundred-fifty big sparkly diva pounds could be a bit conservative. Chuck was big. He was a figure that couldn't be ignored. Somewhere he had learned how to work a room. He was everywhere. He tossed his head back to laugh, making sure to stroke every arm. Kissing every cheek and pretending to listen intently to each word spoken. I couldn't keep my eyes off of him. He was a true showman. Very Liberace.

On the way home, Chuck hooked his arm to mine. He needed the extra support with the buzz and the stilettos wearing him down. The stilettos challenged his every step. We exchanged our regular drunken banter, but Chuck's conversation differed from mine.

"Did you notice the guys at the back table! Oh my god! They were so cute!" He gushed, grabbing a tighter hold on my arm.

He wanted to know my take on the guys he thought were cute. He laughed when I told him I hadn't noticed any guys.

Obviously, we had different things on our minds at the party. He was looking for love in all the wrong places, and I was looking for dip without soggy chip butts in it and a piece of celery without a lipstick bit mark.

They put out some clam dip at one point, but it seemed weird and had an odd color. It scared me when I saw some of the guests double-dipping. The hair on my sweet and sour meatball left me nibbling at pretzels the rest of the evening. Pretzels seemed to be the only safe food in the joint. God only knows where they had been previously, but each handful I grabbed was dry and seemed safe enough. I'm not sure what kind of beer was in the free keg, but I drank my fair share. Since I was pretty screwed up before we arrived, they could have served me saltwater, and I wouldn't have noticed. Eventually, I was able to squint at my phone. With a focused attempt, I read 2:48 AM.

Things became blurry and split in two. Chuck let go of my arm and stumbled on ahead, rambling on about Percy.

Percy was his casual boyfriend. According to Chuck, he was a small Irish fag and a sweet boy. That was the last thing I heard Chuck say that evening.

I remember that it felt like a lightning bolt had shot into the back of my head, moving down my spine and out of my ass. My legs seemed to leave my body. I was on the ground. My left ear pressed against my upper arm. I took a bit of comfort in the fact that my head hadn't slammed into the pavement. It was confusing. I tried to get up, but I couldn't move a muscle. I heard struggling and thumping noises. There were screaming grunts and desperate cries. My eyes would only open to slits. What I managed to see was very blurred, almost as if looking through the bottom of a pink glass. There must have been blood in them.

I saw three figures talking, laughing, and standing around a mass on the ground that I knew was Chuck. They were kicking him. He was curled up in a fetal position crying and begging them to stop. I tried to yell at them, but only a guttural groan followed by a cough came out of my mouth like my mouth was gagged. I have never felt so helpless or completely vulnerable as at that time. It was a living nightmare. I passed out.

When I came to, the first thing I managed was a scream. Chuck lay sprawled out completely naked about two feet in front of me. He was covered in blood from head to toe. His face gashed and swollen. His hair plastered fast against his head with sticky, drying blood. He had a multitude of deep cuts and was covered in dirt and loose gravel. They had stuffed a large clump of the hair from his wig into his mouth, and his clothes were strewn about. They had severed his penis. I was sure he was dead. The lights went out again. The next time I woke was in a hospital emergency room. When I opened my eyes, an unusually bright light assaulted them. My head was pounding, almost as hard as my heart. My thoughts raced to Chuck.

The nurse told me Chuck was in critical condition and had been flown to Harbor View in Seattle. I was relieved to know he was alive. He was one tough motherfucker. I was bandaged and invited to stay the night. I guess they wanted to make sure my head wasn't screwed up any more than usual. It took a few days to find out Chuck would make a recovery. The word full was not included. I'm assuming because certain things don't grow back. He spent a few weeks in the hospital. After his release, he stayed on in Seattle for nearly two months. His mother lived there. She took care of him until he was well enough to come home. I thought that was the best thing for him. What better time to have your mommy.

We spoke nearly every day on the phone during his down-time. He told me that they never found the other half of his penis. He added that they had to look cause they didn't want anyone stumbling upon it by chance. I felt a bit queasy when he half-jokingly suggested a stray dog or cat probably got to it. Chuck opened a fresh warm Diet Coke, which he had to push Boyd's nose away from. He stroked the cat's head and then burped in his face. I had to smile. McHale's Navy was just starting.

5

We Are at War

Size does matter. The total volume has always been of interest since that original eureka moment. Imagine a naked Greek man running through the street shouting, "Eureka!"

He hadn't found a coupon for a complimentary bottle of wine. Archimedes, while sitting in a bathtub, had noticed the water displacement. His discovery was all about figuring out the purity of gold and the actual amount of gold in a given piece of jewelry. The swindle was over for quite a few sneaky jewelers.

The word eureka comes from the Greek word to discover. Likely he ran through the street naked, excited, exuberantly yelling. "I found it. I discovered it."

Heureka(ηευρεκα) from heuriskein (ηευρισκειν): to discover. Our English word heuristic comes to us from this word, which was handed down through the generations. It made its way from Greece heuriskein to Rome heuristicus. The Germans discovered it and gave it a Northern European sound heuristich. The English, who were always eager to borrow smart sounding things from the Germans, turned it into heuristic. Latin, German, and English all pronounce the H as a consonant. Whereas it was generally a vowel in Greek. Something like an eh sound. The E was likely hard, and the u is a lowercase Y which usually has the sound of ih. It probably sounded something like "erica!" as Archimedes ran excited through the streets.

California's motto appropriately uses Eureka in a play on Archimedes's usage of it, the State of California being the gold rush state. In 1848 after the United States had taken possession of the territory from Mexico, gold was discovered. This was an exciting discovery. I am not sure if James Marshall ran naked through the streets like Archimedes. I doubt it, but he must have been just as excited. So it is a beautiful connection to the past for California to use "Eureka" as the state motto.

Typically the etymology of a word would be left to English majors. The word etymology itself is derived from two Greek words. Etumologia (ετυμολογια) means a sense of truth. Etumon is truth, and logia the study of. The truth of the origin of a word is what the study of etymology is about. This is being removed from the curriculum in school these days. It is replaced by the modern slang English; The jive talk of the under-educated and ignorant masses which our public school systems are churning out.

These poorly educated young men and women are told and expected to believe their language is original and not based on anything from the past. This denies them the true sense and knowledge of the rich history that is heard when they utter modern poetry and thoughts. Cutting them off from the past is intentional. It results in irrevocable changes. Knowledge of the history of our country and its roots is lost forever, replaced with new facts based on feelings. Forgetting of the knowledge of the past. Making our youth pliable and easily manipulated is the apparent goal.

We can't stop the hands on the clock as they tick their way three hundred and sixty degrees a minute, three hundred sixty degrees an hour. They tick towards time to wake up. They tick towards time to sleep. They keep on spinning about the face of our watches until they finally stop. Where another clock exists and keeps ticking.

With rare exception, our soul, our identity as human cries

out for contact. The touch of a friend's hand in your hand. The feeling of warmth from a robust sweaty hug. That embrace of reunion when long-lost and finally found lovers reunite. The joy of holding hands with the first girl, not your relation, who lets you take her hand. Will you let it go? Or will you hold on even though it becomes a sweaty mess? You don't let go, do you?

We are losing this. It is an aspect of humanity that we adore. We do. We adore it and we desire it. We need it desperately. Our most stern punishments take the rights away when someone commits a crime. When a person takes away a freedom from another by stealing, violence or trickery, we take their freedom and lock them away. Apart from those who obey the rules of polite society. They no longer have the ability to touch. To feel the skin and smell the breath of those that have not committed horrendous acts. We put them away in prison. They stay away from society inside the walls of their penal institutions where they socialize with others that have committed similar offenses against our culture, our families, and our states.

If they do not learn to coexist in this environment, then we take a step further and confine them utterly alone. We place them in confinement inside confinement. Inside a solitary cell away from any contact with any other living soul's touch or breath. This is the most severe punishment we have without resorting to capital punishment which we reserve for those former members of society that have no redeeming social value as determined in a court of law.

Isolation away from humanity is the most severe punishment we can place on someone who is to remain a living soul.

Being disobedient in the case of the most severe punishment is to be expected. Civil disobedience is expected of decent citizens. When facing tyranny the oppressed lash out. This is human nature. It is natural law.

There is a higher power and the judgment for being civilly disobedient in the face of tyranny, oppression and evil will be judged not only by local magistrates and juries. History will judge these acts long after the events have transpired. God will judge too - if what you do to push back against tyranny doesn't embarrass you in God's sight. Then you have done the right thing. Even if at the present moment you are receiving punishment for it.

When a jury of your peers decides to keep you away from society, that is when there becomes a reason for you to be socially distanced. What we are experiencing now is not a new normal. It is an abhorrent abnormal and we are voluntarily accepting it.

Make no mistake, we are in the middle of a war. Organized criminal activity inside of government and industry is not giving in or leaving any pathway for escape from this battle for our mind. The information war is real. You are in it now, and it is difficult to find the truth. Suppressing facts and putting forth half-truths and lies as truth are the bread and butter of our current information system.

What if we could bend the arrow of time?

Could there be more to it than we've been told?

Is there some balance between the absolute fundamentalist Christian viewpoint of God being yesterday, today, forever; Or the overly simplistic scientific view of time as a simple line moving constantly forward as an arrow shot from a bow some time in the past?

Maybe both of these views are chauvinistic views that are defended by men who have something to lose if their point is not exactly correct.

Is being mistaken such an unforgivable sin?

6

Las Vegas Oysters

Dr. Kelley tells me that my friends are a reflection of my own personal preferences, ideas, and morals. I couldn't disagree more. That may be one of the heftiest loads of bullshit that I have ever heard.

I believe friends happen to you. You don't have the luxury of shopping for them. They aren't hand-picked. They occur during school and church, or while performing everyday activities, and muddling through necessary situations, like work.

Sometimes you might even like the people you are thrust into friendships with. Other times they just fit the circumstances of your life at a given time. Often you kind of like them, or not at all. If you spend enough time with them, they can grow on you, possibly like a cyst, wart, or a cancer.

Once you have certain friends, you learn that they are also split into categories over time.

The first category would be "best friends." a.k.a the close ones. The ones you can trust and would do anything for.

The second category would be "fun friends." You know, the ones you call when you're having a party, picnic, or need someone to go to happy hour with.

The third category would be everyone else that is a step above acquaintance. Don and Jerry come to mind as I continued spilling my soul to the shrink. Who else would listen to me go on and on about stupid bullshit and act interested without laughing?

I met Donna and Jerry under unusual circumstances. I'm not sure whose fault it was that our lives collided. I could have sworn I looked behind me, both over my shoulder and the rearview mirror. Jerry swears he did the same. We both decide to leave our Safeway parking lot spaces simultaneously. Unfortunately, they were across from each other. Not much damage ensued; we were both thankful for that. After a brief chat, we amicably parted ways. I noticed as I pulled away that they seemed like a nice couple. Our time together in this life was both brief and as pleasant as a fender-bender meeting could be.

Three months later, we met again under unusual circumstances. Every summer in Missoula, there are plenty of festivals that take place. One in particular, "The Testicle Festival," is a favorite of Chuck's at the end of July. We attend every year. We walk around eating strange greasy festival cuisine and drink as much beer as we can. Usually, there are strange and random sex acts to witness. It is a something for everyone festival.

We waited in line for a Rocky Mountain oyster when I spotted Donna. I had one of those "I know her, but I don't remember from where" moments. Then I noticed Jerry, and it all came back.

"Hold our place, Chuck. I'm going to say hi to a couple of friends and will be right back."

They were four people ahead of us in line. I wondered if they would recognize me. Instead of being a sane and forthright person and just approaching them, I oped to act like a childish idiot. I walked past the procession of testicle lovers to the vendor's order window menu. I pretended to note a few prices and turned to walk back to Chuck and our place in line, intentionally making myself discernible. I dropped my keys and picked them up. It worked. Jerry had a broad smile and an extended hand.

"Well, fancy meeting you here, stranger!" He said in surprise.

I accepted his shake and gave Donna a hug. I introduced them to Chuck. We ate a deep-fried bull ball together at an incredibly dirty table in the blazing sun. Our lower-end friendship was born.

Donna and Jerry grew to be known as "the couple," not that they always acted like it. Their relationship seems perfect to the unknowing eye. To those of who are blessed to know them, perfect would not be an adjective of choice. They are genuinely two people who can't live without each other, but they should consider giving it a shot.

A few of us took a weekend trip to Las Vegas. Myself, Chuck, his sweet boy Percy, Donna, Jerry, and a friend of theirs named Gina. Thank God it was a quick trip. Who knows what more would have happened if we had stayed any longer. I'll cut to the chase. We did some touristy bullshit, what we could squeeze into two and a half days. One show, four buffets, one hell of a lot of drinking and gambling to taste filled our days up. It was a group effort for the most part.

Jerry and Gina decided to spice things up a bit. Honestly, I saw it coming like a freight train. The trip started out on an upbeat and energized note. We all expected a pleasurable and exciting time. After a group gorging at the Monte Carlo buffet, we decided to drop fifty dollars each into those buck a spin machines. We figured at Georges a pull. Someone was bound to score a decent hit. We were correct. Percy hit and made seven hundred dollars right off the bat. He opted to take the money and run, obviously as bright as he is sweet. We didn't see him or Chuck again until we boarded the plane home. I lost my fifty in four minutes, which is typical for me. I wasn't concerned. I'm what some would refer to as quite comfortable, but I stopped at that loss. I'm also considered by many to be a bit frugal, but the truth in plain English would be that I'm as cheap as any asshole out there, maybe even cheaper.

Donna was doing the button-pushing on the machine. It was one of those that had different sequences of sevens and cherries. Jerry stood behind her, watching for the big pay-off. Jerry is a tall and lanky guy. He has green eyes and dark hair; one of those poor bastards you want to walk up behind and hike up his jeans; no ass. He's not a good-looking guy. Not the type of guy you would expect to see with Donna. Donna is striking; long copper hair, blue eyes, petite, slim, and well dressed. They say opposites attract, and in this case, it appears to be true. I wondered how she stomachs sleeping with him. Don't get me wrong, Jerry is a fun and likable guy; but he looks like the poster boy for all the unattractive bastards out there who don't think they can bag a babe.

I notice that Gina is cruising around, watching others gamble. She is a decent-looking woman; with short dark hair and blue-eyed. I must say, though, she has an ass that could shade half of Texas, shapely yet titanic. From the moment I was introduced to her, I hated her; she immediately came across as a devious, evil bitch. When I saw her approach Donna and Jerry, I had a hunch and hung back a bit, taking it all in.

She glanced my way and gave me a smile that conveyed she didn't care that I was watching or if I saw what she was going to do. I was only half surprised when her hand slid across

Jerry's ass (what he has of one). I was half disgusted that he didn't see a bit fazed by it. He only put a wandering finger behind him and hooked it to one of hers. That was only one of the few moments that I thought my therapy might actually be useful. Who else, besides your shrink, would listen to all this stupid bullshit and act interested, at least without laughing?

Jerry leaned over slightly to give Donna a peck on the cheek. Being enthralled with her two dollars per spin progress, she barely noticed them walk away together. I noticed and was well, too aware. I stayed put and watched her winnings swell. Finally, I took the stool next to hers. We spent the next half hour laughing at wins and groaning each time she lost.

She decided that eight hundred dollars was a sufficient amount to push the collect button. We went to the cashier window to reap her rewards. I accepted her offer of a drink at the bar. I noted how strange it was that she didn't mention Jerry for what I considered a significant amount of time.

As we chatted, she became somewhat edgy. Maybe distracted would be the better word for it. She looked around and responded to questions with a simple "what?" While she squirmed on her seat. I know the signs and why she was fidgeting. She was feeling Jerry's absence, and you could tell it wasn't sitting right with her. Hoping to avoid her inevitable realization, I took a long, smooth gulp while she finished off her gin and soda. She then excused herself to go to her room.

With a noisy "burp," I said, "see ya," and planted a burpy kiss on the cheek Jerry had missed and left to drink my way around Sin City.

I lost some on the slots, took pleasure in another buffet,

and bought a keychain shaped like the MGM Grand lion. It surprised me when there weren't any shot glasses with the name of Boyd stenciled on them. Then I realized how stupid it was that I even thought to look. On that note, I decided to go to my room and take a little nap before embarking on my continued bender at the Hard Rock Cafe.

I resumed the bender, but I never made it to the Hard Rock. When I stepped off of the elevator on my floor, I stood still for a moment to decide which direction to go. This happened every time I went out; I ended up in a different elevator. All the hallways look the same, so it's kind of like completing a maze to get to the room. Soon after picking my path, I realized I had chosen the right one.

Donna was sitting with her back against the wall, outside her and Jerry's door. She looked up at me as I approached. She was shaken, but there were no tears. Standing beside her, I looked, and she met my eyes.

She blurted out. "Jerry's in the room, but he's busy at the moment."

Her mouth tightened, and I managed to say. "I'm sorry." I extended a hand to help her up.

We went into my neighboring room. My first reaction to any sign of adversity, turmoil, or conflict is to pour alcohol. We each cracked a beer fresh out of my bathroom basin filled with cans and cold water. The water was a lot of ice this morning: I like to plan ahead.

The first few moments at the corner table with the ashtray, push-button phone, and hotel stationery were long and awkward. Once she started her tale, it was like the floodgates opened up. She spewed forth much more than I ever thought

I would know about any two people's relationship. Six beers and two hours later, she took a breath. Her eyes squinted, cocking her head to one side, waiting for my input.

There were millions of things I could have said, but I decided to say the wrong thing. I asked her if she would stay with Jerry, and send Gina to hell courtesy of the pointed, sequined toe of her shoe.

I was surprised when she asked me what Gina had to do with it. Fuck, Donna had believed that Jerry was in their room with a hooker. She slammed her beer can on the floor. It was empty and charged for the door. Holy shit, I just sat there listening to the heaviness click shut behind her. I thought about turning on the TV. Then I thought about the time I would have to spend in the witness chair when this debacle was over and drifted off to sleep.

I woke up wondering if my neighbors were still alive, and if so, would they be interested in a final buffet before going to the airport. My bags in hand, I knocked on their door. Jerry opened it a crack. I asked if they were ready to go. He gave me a look I still don't recognize. He ran an open palm from the middle of his face all the way back to the top of his head. In a flat tone, he informed me that they would meet me in the lobby in forty-five minutes. I headed for my final buffet before going to the airport.

I sat and waited an additional twenty-five minutes for them to show up at checkout. I had decided I would leave for the plane after thirty. They finally showed up looking quite sober. Gina was nowhere to be seen. We boarded the airport shuttle and barely made our flight.

As I approached my seat, Chuck and Percy waved and

smiled. As only two keyed-up divas with purses full of newly acquired cash could. I had to laugh. Thank God I had two normal friends. Donna and Jerry made it home together intact as a couple. We never saw Gina again or ever mentioned her. I guess what happens in Vegas, really does stay there.

7

Excess Moisture

Dr. Kelley suggested we talk a bit about my lifestyle. She was aware of my inherited wealth, as well as my substantial case of thriftiness. At first, I wasn't sure where we were headed with this one. It ended up going down a road I wasn't too keen on traveling. I could literally sense the pending questions. She wanted to know why I didn't work. It was the first bullet I had to dodge. I explained that my working would take a perfectly good job away from some poor bastard that might actually need it. I was pretty exultant with that answer; it made me sound somewhat noble. I wasn't quite sure if she bought it, but I stated it so well, I almost did.

She then asked why I didn't volunteer. That one was a bit tougher. I realized that was a bullet I was going to have to take. I couldn't think of one reason, on the spot like that, to justify my lack of charity. I simply had to fess up. I confessed my shortage of motivation and laziness. Until I heard myself say the words, I wasn't even aware of what a selfish asshole. I guess she brought me to a personal reality. I couldn't help notice her nose wrinkle as her eyebrows dipped down in a poorly muted look of disgust. I started doing some obvious fidgeting. I could feel the heat rising in my cheeks, both sets. I was pretty sure there would be a sweat line where my ass crack was on that skanky old couch when I got up.

She composed her expression before she went on to explain. Helping others, not only benefits mankind. It also could raise my sense of self-worth and personal satisfaction. The doc continued for what I considered way too long. She made several suggestions on how I could serve the community. I felt more like I was at a seminar on achieving sainthood than at a therapy session.

It was suggested that I could volunteer at the old folks' home. Clean cages at Animeals, which was a local animal shelter and food bank. Maybe shop for the disabled? Pick up litter in the local parks. Help out at the homeless shelter. Pick the noses of those with no fingers. Wipe the asses of the populace afraid of fecal matter, and on and on, and on and freaking on. At that point, all I wanted to do was get the hell out of there. Dab the excess moisture off my ass and possibly change my underwear.

Chuck and I are having a few drinks at Curley's happy hour. I realize he is hot on the trail to completely shit-faced. He started to light a smoke. Even after noticing he had the wrong end in his mouth, I let him proceed. After searing the filter into an unusable lump, he swore and pulled a few stray tobacco bits off of his tongue. I laughed and reminded him of the no-smoking policy. Then I quickly waved at the annoyed server, assuring him that the situation was under control. What a stench that thing put off. Of course, the incident sparked the whole public smoking debate. Chuck didn't seem to care that I was agreeing with him. He argued with me anyway. Then he attempted to suck the people at the neighboring table into the dispute.

He looked in their direction and loudly slurred. "Don't you think if you own an establishment, you should be the one to decide if people can smoke it?! HA! I mean in it!"

They pretended not to hear him and continued minding their own business. He looked back at me and shrugged his meaty shoulders. I aggressively changed the subject.

"I was instructed to find a cause to support." I blurted, desperate to pique his curiosity.

This only received a blank uninterested stare. I went on to explain.

"My therapist suggested it. She said it would improve my self-esteem and self-worth, you know, bullshit like that."

His expression remained uninterested. Then he suddenly threw his head back and purged a huge belly laugh. He came at me with a thick mocking tone.

"I can see it now." Gesturing with his plump hands. "You making tuna or bologna sandwiches for homeless people downtown every weekday afternoon. Packing them into paper lunch sacks decorated with Hello Kitty!"

After a long snort, a huge swig of beer, and a rancid burp, he continued, and I let him.

"You could add snack bags of Doritos and airplane-sized bottles of scotch! A lot of homeless are also alcoholics and might get the munchies." He concluded.

I called him a fucking smart ass. He agreed with a nod and another gulp of brew. So we continued to laugh. It's pretty amazing what booze can disguise as funny.

After I confirmed his inebriated condition, I decided I could talk him into anything. The only problem now would be if he remembered it tomorrow. I went ahead and spewed a boatload of garbled bullshit about the point at hand. I was going to make a contribution to the community, and he was gonna join me on my journey. Misery loves company.

The next morning I woke with a gigantic mass of brown fur sprawled across my neck. It wasn't surprising being as restricted breathing is what woke me up. I pried Boyd off of my airway, yawned, and tried to clear my head. Recalling the previous evening, I guessed Chuck was in a nearby jail cell.

Yet another gigantic mass passed out on my skanky couch. I headed out into the front room. I was relieved to see his fat, snoring ass fast asleep, face down in an end cushion. Boyd woke him with a sandpaper tongue lick to the ear. Chuck pushed the cat away with his open palm. He followed with a loud fart and a strained grunt. Hoisting himself up into a seated position, he smiled a hung-over smile. I went to the fridge and pulled out a Diet Coke for him. He was appreciative of the gesture, even though the can was chilled. He took a huge swig, followed by a deafening burp. I knew what was coming next. There would be a lineup of morning-after questions. That guy has no head for alcohol.

He started with the usual. "Did I meet someone? Did you meet someone? Did we go to Taco John's?"

I told him we didn't meet anyone or eat anything. He seemed to breathe a small sigh of relief. I continued and reminded him that he agreed to volunteer with me. He took another gulp of soda. I think he incorporated the word fuck into his second gut-busting belch. Boyd bounded off the couch. He stood up and walked towards the bathroom, "You're a fucking asshole. I gotta take a dump."

We were on our way to community service.

I explained to Percy that Chuck and I were looking for a community cause to support. At least I was looking for a cause. Chuck was just along for the ride, like it or not. I needed him for support. Percy's reaction didn't surprise me. His unibrow raised, much higher than I thought physically possible. Then he delivered a predictable speech. He began by professing his love and admiration for Chuck. This was quickly followed up with the fact that Chuck is extremely self-centered and unusually lazy. On that, we agreed. This wasn't going to be easy.

It only took a few seconds to realize that Chuck's only interest was, well, Chuck. It shocked us when we both comprehended that at the same time. After all, was said and done, we agreed. This would be more beneficial to Chuck than either of us had imagined.

The following morning I struggled up the outside staircase to Chuck's apartment. Knocking politely before letting myself in. I passed his prim, proper, potpourri bullshit on my way to his bedroom. I was quite sure of the scenario I would be walking into. A huge snoring, sweaty lump, concealed in 1800 thread count Ralph Lauren bed sheets, and last night's Skyy vodka mixed with stale rancid farts. It was an accurate prediction. I gave him a firm poke on the shoulder. Nothing … It crossed my mind that he could be dead. Then he snorted and rolled over. He opened his bloodshot eyes, wincing. It was the reaction you'd want when you're the first sight of someone's day.

He greeted me with a raspy and productive cough. Then he asked me what the fuck I wanted. I sat down on the edge of the bed. My weight caused him to roll towards me. His mid-drift spare tire bounced onto my thigh.

I asked, "Wanna go have breakfast? I'm payin'."

No hangover in the world would keep Chuck from a free meal. I knew that for a fact.

We sat down at a semi-clean table in Ruby's cafe. Chuck was wearing his sunglasses. They would remain on throughout the entire artery-hardening repast. I was glad. The last thing I wanted to see was his bloody, uninterested stare while I explained our new volunteer duties. I attempted to eat my runny egg yolks, but thinking about his eyes made my stomach turn. Guess I was a little hungover myself, but I pressed on.

What do you do with a drunken faggot? With Percy's approval, my idea was to help out at the local nursing home. Chuck's initial reaction was less than enthusiastic. He wanted to back out. I reminded him of his promise to escort me on my journey to self-improvement. I could smell the hate and alcohol secreting out of his pores. I wasn't going to let this fat fucking fish off of the hook. He was gonna follow through on something. I was going to benefit; he was going to benefit, and all the patients at the home were going to benefit. All our lives would be fuller and more meaningful from the experience; God damn it.

We walked through the heavily smudged glass double doors together. The irregular smell hit me first; I felt my nose involuntarily scrunch towards my eyebrows. Chuck gave me a look, not a friendly look. It was one of those short, warning-packed glances; my skin crawled.

We walked up to the reception desk. A skinny, old ugly woman was seated behind it. She gave us an unwelcoming stare. I wanted to grab Chuck by the sleeve, turn and run. I didn't, but I probably should have. Then suddenly, I was astounded. Chuck folded his huge feminine fingers into a proper pile and plopped them squarely in front of the ratty-looking old bitch and her outdated computer. Then he delivered a warm introduction on behalf of both of us.

"Hello Ma'am, We have an appointment to volunteer today!"

His cheerful confidence continued. He assured her that we were there to help in any way necessary, and we were happy to do so. I wasn't sure whether to puke, laugh or applaud.

We were led down a long hallway to a door labeled director. We looked at each other with the expression two kids may have before entering the principal's office. Chuck tapped the frosted glass of the door window lightly with his knuckles.

"Come in," a voice bolstered from within.

Chuck turned the knob and pushed the door open. We walked in. A small gray-haired man was sitting behind a desk. He looked like a sweet little grandpa. Looks can be deceiving.

Chuck took the initiative. He strode forward, with his hand extended towards the directors's desk. His gesture wasn't reciprocated. I wasn't sure if I should be embarrassed or pissed off. Chuck dropped the intended handshake to his side, immediately launching into an obvious aggravated yet composed introduction.

He then continued with a detailed list of reasons explaining our interest in volunteering at this fine establishment. His spiel was full of creative and insane compliments, peppered with fabricated concerns for the elderly and disabled. It was all complete bullshit. I knew he was doing it all for me. I was reminded of why he was my best friend. I definitely needed a reminder from time to time. As touched as I was, I didn't try and interject. I skipped any form of assistance. I was ashamed of myself but decided to live with it.

Marvin Quinn listened to Chuck's banter without interruption. When he was sure Chuck was finished, he opened a heavy desk drawer and pulled out a worn clipboard. We were instructed to follow him. He hobbled towards the door, clipboard under his armpit and a well-worn cane in his shaky aged hand. Chuck offered me a condescending smile before turning to follow Marvin, the miser. We were about to experience a well guided reluctant tour of Blushing Meadows Nursing Home.

Sundays would never be the same.

8

Pretty Pink Fingernails

I'm sitting in Dr. Kelley's office, overwhelmed with the anticipation of her arrival. Every time I get here early, I'm presented with way too much time to think. I ask myself why I come here, on my own accord, and feel like I'm about to have a tooth extracted. Then I try to analyze my way of thinking. Not easy. I seem to come to the same conclusion each time. I tell myself that talking to her is a way of venting very confidentially. She is paid to listen, advise, and keep her big judgmental mouth full of only things I want to hear. Well, that's what I wish she would do. I'm still amazed that I schedule another appointment, without hesitation, before I leave.

She enters the room with the usual smile plastered on her face and eases herself into the high-backed office chair. I'm smiling too, wondering how much my ass has contributed to the dent in this couch cushion. The usual banter ensues, pleasantries, and the same old rhetorical questions. Then the real shit begins.

"So, last time we spoke, we discussed you possibly doing some volunteer work. Have you given that any consideration yet?"

I sensed she was expecting a slew of excuses as to why I hadn't. There was a considerable amount of surprise, maybe disbelief, in her expression when I answered. I went on to tell the whole sordid Blushing Meadows story.

I explained Chuck's initial reluctance. I told her how he ended up coming through for me. I raved on his behalf for taking charge at the home. I gushed about how impressed I was with his ability to stand up for himself and his friend in an adverse situation. I now see that instead of appreciating my allegiance towards my friend, she saw it as some red flag.

She cut off my Chuck praising rampage and began questioning me about how many friends, past or present, have let me down. I was taken back a bit. I wasn't sure where this was all headed. She let out a breathy sigh and cocked her head to one side. She continued to explain her surprise at how Chuck's display of loyalty seemed exceptional to me. I must admit, I was unsure why myself. I hadn't realized that it was a foreign experience. I told her, without uncertainty, that none of my friends had ever let me down. Nor had any ever thrown me under the bus. It was at that point; I realized none had ever stepped up to the plate for me either. That was a whole other session.

I did have memories of people that screwed me over pretty well. None of them were friends. I wondered if she cared about the other categories of assholes. I suddenly flashed back to a particular acquaintance. It was a few years ago. I had a day all to myself. It started with sleeping in 'til about 10 am. I then proceeded with the usual daily routine, not to be skipped. I filled up Boyd's kibbles, scooped the kitty litter box, picked up fur balls, and cleaned puke spots. I didn't feed myself because I planned on having lunch out that day.

I was sitting in a booth at Denny's, waiting for my meal. I love the food at Denny's. Sure, everything on the menu tastes the same, but the price is right. I had forgotten the newspaper and had already read the Carte du jour. So I decided to people watch and eavesdrop instead.

I quickly noticed these two guys in the booth across from mine - skanky-looking bastards, to say the least. They weren't nearly as quiet as they should have been, considering the content of their conversation. They bantered back and forth about the price of an ounce of pot that some other asshole had brought back from Seattle. At least that's what I believed I heard. I was distracted by the waitress refilling my watery coffee. Her huge frame and fat lumpy ass blocked them entirely from my view. After a thankful nod for the refill, I wrenched my neck to see around her. When she finally waddled away, the show continued.

I could see four hands under their table doing a very fluid brail-like exchange. Nice and smooth. They got up and left the table. I could smell the stench of body odor, pot, and stale Pall Malls in the wake of air as they passed by. They left a hefty mess, but no tip. What a couple of cheap assholes. There I was, sitting feeling bad for the big butt waitress that didn't get a tip. I should have been more concerned that two boils on the ass of society just made a drug deal in an American institution. I like Denny's.

Truthfully, to my admitted shame, there was a time when I wasn't considered much better. Maybe I'm still not, but I am a good tipper. Today I'm probably just more cautious or too chicken shit to take the chances the youth find no big deal.

My mind raced back to a guy I knew named Billy. I ate my superbird sandwich and grease-laden, ketchup-drenched french fries. Then I recalled more than I cared to about a horrifically unforgettable night.

Billy was by far the biggest fucking asshole I had ever met. I was going to say in the world, but I hadn't all the world's fucking assholes. So dubbing him the biggest would almost be giving him an honor. Honors were not something he deserved. Billy was the kind of guy anyone would have loved to see get his throat slit. I'm sure more than a few individuals considered doing just that. Billy would sell you a car at a great price and steal it back before signing over the title. He would beat his dog for taking a shit in the house after being locked in it for three or more consecutive days. Billy's girlfriend always had a black eye or some sort of facial abrasion.

The two of us met about fifteen years before through a mutual acquaintance. At the time, it seemed a necessary union. Billy had the best shit a die-hard smoker could ask for. Don't get me wrong; the pot wasn't for personal use. I already had plenty of bad habits under my belt. I smoked cigarettes, drank like a fish, ate like a pig, and swore like a sailor. Enough is enough. Besides, the cost was ridiculous. That was why Billy and I formed our twisted alliance. I saw the opportunity to profit from the pathetic addictions of those willing to pay almost anything for just one more hit. I became the "middleman, profiteer extraordinaire."

Billy's girlfriend at the time was named Allison. She went by Ally. She was a gorgeous girl with mousy brown hair and beautiful big green eyes. Usually, one of which was encased in a ring of black. I didn't understand her attraction to that stupid prick. I'm guessing she may have questioned it a time or two herself. The three of us met one evening for a lot of drinks. For what could potentially be a mutually lucrative business deal. We sat at a table in the corner of the bar. I instantly noticed the band-aid perched over Ally's right eyebrow. I shook my head slightly and laughed to myself in honor of the sheer idiocy of their relationship. We talked about unrelated bullshit, ate deep-fried chips dipped in a slightly discolored guacamole, then downed about eight shots of scotch each.

We got down to business. Billy decided to tickle my frugality bone. He convinced me to buy a substantially more significant amount of product than I had initially intended. He explained how the larger quantity would lower my investment price, thus increasing my overall profit by as much as a fourth. I was sold.

The new plan required going for a ride. We piled into Billy's rust-riddled 1972 ford pick-up. Ally sat in the middle.., singing to a Dolly Pardon song barely leaking out of the static-ridden radio. She sounded pretty good. Good old Billy always had a stash of Coors on the passenger side of his rig. We all cracked one open. Nobody seemed to care that they were piss warm. I was a bit surprised at the fact I was having a good time, not something you usually experience around Billy. The ride was far from smooth. Between the shitty shocks and abundant potholes, we did some serious seat leaping and laughing. It's amazing what becomes funny when you're full of scotch and tepid beer. We hit a bump that sent Billy's Coors can crashing into his top teeth so hard we were pretty sure it had become a permanent dental fixture. Ally laughed until booze was oozing out of her nose. Then I think she may have switched to crying. It must have hurt. She recovered quickly and continued drinking.

We continued on, swilling and driving, then came to a railroad crossing. A dizzying wave of panic washed over me when our back tires wouldn't clear the tracks. By the looks on my companion's faces, I think they experienced the same feeling. My first instinct was to get out of the truck. I lit a cigarette and walked around to the driver's side. His window was open, so I leaned in to discuss our situation delay. I was amazed to see Billy had his seatbelt on and equally surprised that my drunk ass noticed. I definitely sensed his nervousness as he fumbled while trying to unfasten it.

The moment I heard it click open, I saw a beaming light coming towards us. It was surreal and seemingly out of nowhere. I'm guessing Billy saw it, too, just based on the sheer force behind the truck door when he pushed it open. It sent me flying to a very ungraceful landing several feet back. Billy was out and running before I could struggle back onto my feet. The pain had no description. I lifted my face towards the pick-up and saw Ally, still sitting in the middle of the bench seat. I bet it's safe to assume that those pretty green eyes had never been that wide open before. She must have been paralyzed by her fear, that and a lot of less than premium alcohol. She never moved. The light was upon us. I dove to the left and rolled away; again, I had to fight my way back to an upright position. The impact was unparalleled. I had never heard a noise like it before, hope I never do again. I knew I was alive, only because I turned my head to see the sight of my life. There were sparks, smoke, and fire. The screeching of the train brakes and steel scraped along steel was deafening. I froze for a few minutes. I just stood there in awe. The trauma and my drunken state made it near impossible to remain standing. I'm not sure how I managed it. I did a lot of staggering as I walked towards the wreckage. The train dragged the truck at least a few hundred feet down the tracks.

My perception and judgment were less than fine-tuned that evening. I felt like I was getting close when I fell, hard. My face took the hit that my hands should have. I used all the strength I had in my arms to lift myself enough to pull my cheek off of a protruding rock. It didn't seem to hurt. I rolled myself onto my ass and just sat there a few minutes. At least it felt like a few minutes, not sure.

As I sat, my vision began to clear; I hadn't even realized it was blurred. I leaned forward to prepare to stand again. My left hand landed on something soft. I looked down to discover it was resting on what resembled another hand. It was small and had lovely pink fingernails. It sported a petite jade ring on the index finger, not unlike the one Ally was wearing that evening. As I followed my natural line of sight, I noticed the hand was connected to an arm. A partial torso and a neck followed. No head. I wondered what had happened to those beautiful green eyes. My head was spinning, and I threw up. I woke in the ambulance to paramedics looming over me. I could smell vomit inside the oxygen mask they had strapped to my face. They asked me questions, not sure if they were supposed to do that. I couldn't answer anyway. I still can't believe that in the midst of all that horror, confusion, and sadness, I could lay there with selfish, trivial thoughts. I thought how glad I was that I hadn't given Billy any money yet, can you believe that?

Several years after that fateful night, I saw Billy again. He didn't see me. I watched the stupid fucking jerk sit alone, eating his Wendy's hamburger with one hand. His right arm was missing from the shoulder. I knew it didn't happen in the accident. That pussy was probably snuggled up in his bed before the train struck the Ford. I really hoped that cocksucker was right-handed.

9

The Golden Years

The Lord, my God, does not need a great house or altar. He couldn't, for the creator of everything must know that nothing, not even a temple, the size of a mountain would matter. To the creator of the mountains, how would something manmade from the resources of those mountains? The temple of the creator is his creation. The sandcastle that man may build could never compare to the temple that the Creator has created for himself. Man is best served to build not temples to God but to build sanctuary and homes for fellow men. This is truly the best way to serve God.

There is nothing more important than family. It's the reason up to half the country is willing to work sometimes double and triple jobs to ensure their family can live properly. Eating the right foods and going to the schools that will teach them to become independent, successful citizens. We have an obligation to work hard to ensure the succeeding generation has complete and total control of their destiny.

When a parent sees a blooming child become something, to become successful, this is the beauty of the creation of God. Who could stop to imagine anything other than the opportunities that await our kids? They will open new and exciting doors, behind which lie both traps and treasures. I pray that the treasures await my children.

There are traps, entanglements, and tortures that will befall most, if not all before there is any treasure to recover. Certainly, the lucky few gather the most. If you fall into the majority, that has to work hard, being diligent, and tough. You are a winner in life too. It's a long way to the top, and there is a ton of hard work along the way. If you are not willing to work hard, then don't expect to get success along the way.

**

I was feeling apprehensive as I leaned against the front of the building. With every minute that passed, I was convinced that I would be stood up. My mind argued with itself. The positive thinking side of my brain told me that Chuck was a good friend and would never let me down. I could imagine seeing his flaming, glorious self come bounding around the corner at any second. The realistic side reminded me that he was a narcissistic, selfish, and lazy asshole, that he wouldn't think twice about blowing me off to sleep in. Then I was pissed. That son of a bitch wasn't coming. Then panic set in. What if he didn't show? Could I walk in and fulfill my obligations alone? After all, I dragged him into this steaming pile of crap just so I wouldn't have to do it alone. Fuck, I wished that I had a smoke. I couldn't believe how close I was to having a full-blown panic attack. I decided to flee the scene. Just as I began to descend the stairs, I heard his obnoxiously loud, overly enthusiastic morning greeting. I sighed in relief and immediately regretted it. Why hadn't I decided to leave a few minutes earlier?

Our first Sunday at Blushing Meadows began with force-feeding octogenarians and quadriplegics nutritiously balanced breakfasts. Then we were handed bus tubs and transformed into cafeteria custodians. I was hoping for an early dismissal, but it wasn't to be. Our last task was to pay a friendly and stimulating visit to a lonely old lady. That sounded easy enough.

Carole Stapleton lived in room 212. She was our assigned

resident. We would visit her every week for an hour before leaving the home. We were informed that Carole had spent the previous fifteen years inside room 212. The past ten of which had been without a single visitor. It became obvious quickly as to why.

I followed Chuck into her room. She was sitting next to a half-open window in a chair made of beautifully stained wood. I thought it odd that the chair didn't have a cushion. I tend to notice weird shit like that.

She was tiny, her hair pure white and short, hosted a few remnants of an ancient perm. As we entered her domain, she turned her attention from the outside view to us. The lack of cushion allowed her to slide easily in our direction. She looked at us as intruders; I guess we were. Chuck decided to continue with his new role as the initiative taker. He rushed towards her; arms open wide. I can only imagine what must have been going through her head at that moment. He gave her what we call the "air" embrace. Arms fully extended around the subject, with absolute minimum physical contact. Which was like a four-finger tap on the back. He surprised me when he grabbed her skinny white and very bony hands on his way back to an upright position, declaring Carole the cutest thing he'd ever seen.

She pulled her hands away as abruptly as a ninety-something crone can manage. I will never forget or be able to describe Chuck's face when she told him to keep his big queer mitts to himself. I must confess to being pleasantly surprised by this outcome. This could turn out to be fun. Nope...

Chuck let forth his most profuse apology. I could tell she was enjoying his embarrassed nervousness. After a bit of cajoling, she agreed to let us stay and chat for a while. By the end of our allotted hour, we knew a hell of a lot about Carole Stapleton, who was a dismal piece of shit extraordinary. She was in the mood to let us in on every miserable moment of her life, from conception to the present day.

Carole was born to a pig farmer, Archy, and his wife Anna about four hundred years ago. They had immigrated to Anoka, Minnesota, from Norway about three hundred years before that. Carole informed us that the shit of her life hit the fan from the first memory in her head. This crazy old bitch was one for the books. I wished Dr. Kelley could be here. As apprehensive as I was, Chuck seemed enthralled with her American story.

In a nutshell, Carole's father had been an alcoholic and indulged in several extramarital affairs. According to his wife, most of them were with various prized livestock. Her mother, on the other hand, had been a staunch Christian. Both a bible beater and a child beater as well. The story became garbled to me; the lack of interest, disbelief, and sheer disdain at Chuck's undivided attention made me sick. She shared her reasons for the lack of visitations. My ears perked up. Carole had six children. The paternity of these individuals was in question and obviously, at this point, would remain so. Carole shared with us the fact that her late husband John was a generous man. He would have given his buddy the shirt off his back or even his wife if they requested.

Carole's firstborn was Sarah. Carole described her as one of the ugliest girls she had ever seen. Hence, she was quite relieved when Sarah found someone to marry. He was an equally challenged man when it came to looks. They were on their way to a new life together in Eugene, Oregon, when they both died in a head-on collision. Carole shrugged her shoulders and offered that it may have been for the best. Their children would have surely been nothing short of beastly. I noticed Chuck's eyes widen at the remark, which caused me to catch a silent giggle at the hilarious absurdity of her statement. Jeffery was her second child. He was born only ten months after Sarah. Carole said she was overjoyed that he was a handsome baby. Unfortunately, he turned out to be what she described as a full-fledged retard. Jefferey was institutionalized at the age of five and died of pneumonia at fourteen.

Chuck's eyebrows furrowed, and his look became intense. I tried not to laugh. Tessa was the third in the line of utter catastrophe. She was a beautiful, active and intelligent child. She lived to the ripe old age of seventeen. Carole doesn't recommend ice fishing close to the spring thaw. Stella succumbed to the cold, attempting to save herself on the slippery edge of ice she had fallen through. Death by drowning is only an afterthought when you are already turning into an ice cube.

Ella and Andrew were born together; they would have been numbers four and five had they been live births. I thought about how lucky those two may have been.

Caleb was the last inauspicious infant to be shot from the old bags loins. I was happy to hear that to this day; he is alive and well. Although, according to Carole, he was an ungrateful asshole that doesn't feel the need to visit his poor old decrepit mother. She didn't elaborate on it, but I can imagine he is probably a decent guy with a life. That life doesn't need the grief of a crazy old miserable bitch telling him how lucky he is to be alive.

Before she could break into another unbelievable, strangely heart-wrenching batch of bullshit, unsuccessfully disguised as an entertaining story, I broke it up. I had enough of her psychobabble and reminded Chuck of the time. He shot me an annoyed look because obviously, he was enjoying this fucking crap. I wanted to have lunch.

We stopped to eat on the way home. I was happy to be sitting. My legs were tired from the first morning of volunteer work. Chuck started gushing about how happy and fun his day had been. Between urges to kick his ass, I thought I might even be happy for him. He was experiencing what Dr. Kelley had intended for me.

1 0

Gasolina

This is the single man meeting the gas giant Gasolina. The pressure and weight-bearing down will cause him to succumb to the relentless pressure. There are some situations to which man must surely submit.

There has always been that place avoiding leaves a temptation in the back of your conscience, the place where only the bad things are. It doesn't take science to make you realize that it is in the best interest of health and your mental wellbeing to stay away. It's not difficult, as long as you remain in a conscious mind as you make your way towards that ending place where you rest your head at the end of the day.

I have noticed, unfortunately, that most folks let life flow by. They are flowing through the day, just droning away. That is not a particularly good use of the limited time we have available. In the empty set, nothing good will come of time wasted. It is unfortunate that we have not been given a do-over button. In fact, recently, all of the buttons have been removed. So we move through our days buttonless and not paying any bit of mind to the amazing world passing us by. Sure, with a bit of social training, it is not hard to fake it and stay awake or appear awake during the day.

Normal men spend over 90%, actually approaching 99% of their consciousness, totally unconscious. So much for staying away from those places where we are certain to find trouble. It's practically destiny that the average man will end up in trouble. Drunk and lost when he heads out for an evening of fun with cash in his pocket and an exciting new city in front of him - heading for the shiny neon lights of the nearby district of ill repute that almost every big town across the world has.

Some countries have built their economies around the massive amount of hard currency that is generated at night by naive young men, alcohol, and women. Trouble is certain if there are enough of these three in one place at one time. Left without guidance, men will be in, or cause substantial havoc when enough alcohol and women are around.

There's nothing wrong with taking your friend out for a few beers. That behavior is socially acceptable. That's what good buds do. Buddies go drinking and become so drunk that all decisions seem to be the best choice. There is an opportunity to meet young ladies with the same interests as young men. Tequila shots and lap dances are an undesirable way to get to know a girl.

It seems that men will never learn that lesson. The women will never give up trying to trip the men and attack like ravenous hyenas. This is the reality of young men and women. They are like the hyena. Their behaviors are somewhat similar. The young women manipulate the young men as the hyena female controls the relationship when a pair of hyenas mate.

It all begins on payday when the young man is released to the wild by his employer. He heads out into Friday evening with his hair combed, shoes shined, and pocket bulging with a month's toil, swollen to the bursting point. This young man has a great weekend waiting for him.

"What could go wrong?" He says to himself.

Feeling invincible is a weakness. It is one of the weakest conditions men are afflicted with. It's how you get into bad situations.

Obviously, nobody in their right mind will walk into a robbery. Staying away from the bad guys and bad situations is wise. It makes sense. Men afflicted with invincibility walk right in. They are not looking for trouble. Normally they don't pay attention to the signs and portends that could steer them away from a fight or a robbery. It's not the man's fault. Most of these fights and robberies have something to do with or have been stimulated by women. I'm sure that in many of the cases concerning the women involved, the female did not want to be fought over. They would not have condoned robbery in their name.

Every now and then, that special girl comes along. You have all seen or met the type. That woman that appears to orchestrate the terror. Who seems to be stimulated by and feeding on the violence and crimes achieved by men. Men who fight, commit crimes, and sometimes die to impress or get the attention of the lady of their dreams.

Sure many of the women who are indirectly responsible for the crimes of passion and even premeditated crimes may be completely innocent and ignorant of the violence that may result from their behavior. Their actions, being the actions of young girls, are the source of the biological threat that causes men to lose their minds and turn against common sense.

Later in life, if they have survived their first dozen or so ordeals with falling in love, rejection, disease, love, and marriage, not to mention divorce. Then they might just make it. Even though men finally understand what is going on with life, it doesn't mean they have followed the correct path. They know the right thing to do and which is the appropriate path. That doesn't mean they will follow it. It is the destiny of man to forever make the same mistakes over and over again. It has been said that expecting a different result from the same actions means that you're crazy. If that is the case, then most men are crazy.

Men are going through life continually and constantly taking out their manhood. Getting it slammed in the door by women they have fallen in love forever with. The important thing is the survival of the species. For sure, men are doing a great job of ensuring that there will be a posterity to inherit the earth from.

Although most men have no sense to stop repeating the same mistakes over and again. It is only useful and right to warn them. Do not expect to have your warning followed. Oh sure, they will acknowledge that they have heard you. They will express thanks for the good advice. Usually, they will apologize for not listening to your previous advice. You will be assured it won't happen again. They have learned their lesson. "Bros before hoes," and all that.

Nothing is so special about a woman to live through the aftermath of their wrath, fury, and vengeance. In fact and practice, why it is so horrible is because the man is never told why at least not the real reason. Your friend will sit in a psychedelic blue funk, knowing you warned him and promising not to do it again. You know he will though, and so will you. It is man's destiny.

Maybe today would be the day. He had only one experience under his belt. At least only one to which he would admit. Yeah, there had been other encounters. The dark times in his past. Never admitted to yet still moments that exist in his memory. Embarrassed, overpowered, was it consensual? Time held firm the memories clearly, never to be forgotten. There were no longer hatred-filled moments, just past times, and everyone has a past. He didn't dwell on those moments anymore.

Recently, forgiveness came into thinking, although only momentarily. The rest of the time, no, he wouldn't forgive them. Rape is a horrid crime, and a male victim is in the worst position. Reporting male rape is going to ruin your life and reputation. He held his silence, and when he thought on the subject, his stomach burned. They had been older, bigger, and mean. Most of them were already put away and gone. Society tends to find the way to separate the bad apples from the normal Joes.

Today there is absolutely nothing wrong with him. In fact, the testosterone meter is up towards average American caveman level. He wants meat and a lady. Which lady? Any girl? No! He wants her. The woman that won't stop haunting his sweaty night-terror-filled dreams. He won't rest until he calls her "mine."

I I

The Immortal

When our young man recovers his senses the following day, he will find the number missing a digit, to messy to read. This requires another trip back to the establishment. Gasolina is an irresistible force. Our young man has fallen in love. There is no turning back.

Round two of our young man at the exotic dancer cultural exchange bar will have our man start out more prepared. By evening, his hangover will have subsided. He will have had time to analyze what happened the previous evening. This time he has made sure to bring a notepad and proper pen. He would have been able to read Gasolina's phone number if he hadn't given her a damp napkin and a bowling pencil to write it on. It's Saturday night, and the young man is on his way back to Xanadu. It's going to be a great night.

She knows he will return, being a professional in the twilight of her career. She is as beautiful as an early autumn day. Gasolina is savvy and savory. The evening has already been orchestrated, prepared to complete the withdrawal of the young man's paycheck. That is, the portion of his check she was not able to withdraw before closing time the previous evening. Actually, she thought. "He is kind of cute."

This one might be the replacement for her babies' daddy, who she is not even certain fathered her twins. It is interesting how the genetics of non-identical twins can be. It doesn't matter because she loved both of her children equally.

Laqueesha, with her long blond hair and freckles, was an ebony goddess. It was hard to believe that she was already thirteen. Her boyfriend had taken the whole family to the Sizzler for all you can eat buffet in his Prius station wagon. He had even let Tyrone order off of the menu, in addition to grazing from the salad bar. Tyrone, a gawky redhead and already 6'2", was often confused as Laqueesha's boyfriend, not her brother. His hair was nappy. His skin was a flawless white. Just as white as the toilet he was conceived on top of.

She still regretted that evening, even though she had enjoyed it so much. The fifty dollars was long gone, but she would always have her two angels.

Laqueesha's boyfriend, Scott, was still married, but he seemed so sincere. When Gasolina had confronted him and insisted that Laqueesha remain a virgin. Scott and Laqueesha had both agreed to follow the 33% rule to keep her virginity until the high school prom. That being said, she hoped that Laqueesha could make it to the Prom and even graduate high school. She hadn't been that lucky. Every day she said her prayers and begged the Lord Jesus for forgiveness. This likely being the only smart thing she did consistently.

Throughout her adult life, she thought of herself as a good person, even though she sinned often in order to feed her kids. She always confessed her sins to the Lord Jesus and begged for forgiveness. It was the only way she could reconcile the fact that she basically stole men's money. Every night while sitting on their laps entertaining them for a short time. Maybe it wasn't really stealing; most would remember her forever. Many of those men left with a stain that would remind them of their limited encounter with Gasolina. How can you assign a value to a happy memory?

How many women set out like Gasolina to capture and domesticate a man? When I say man, I am not discussing a random man. I am talking about singling out an unwitting soul for premeditated matrimony.

When a woman such as Gasolina sets her sights on a man, there is nothing that man can do. He must be willing to join the witness protection program or maybe move off to another country. Perhaps he could join the circus and wear a clown disguise. Where he might find a way to escape marital bliss. When a woman this determined has set her eye on an unsuspecting man. Gasolina's acquisition system had locked on her prey. Her next victim did not stand a chance.

Gasolina was practiced in the art of nuptials. Her last four ex-husbands would be worth interviewing if they could be contacted. None of them could afford to pay a phone bill in addition to eating after their divorces from her matrimonial bliss.

"He is just perfect." She thought.

Young, with no baggage, makes him perfectly trainable. He appeared to be so perfect that he looked absolutely yummy. "Yummy, not gummy." She giggled to herself.

He might be worth keeping permanently. What an unbelievable turn of events this could be. The formidable Gasolina was actually falling in love. For the very first time, the tables were being reordered. Another way of looking at reality was becoming available. In the past, men, many men had fallen in love with the ever-beautiful Gasolina. She had never had the same feeling for any of the men that had helped keep the lady in her home.

The only thing more dangerous than a woman scorned is a woman in love. Gasolina had set her mind on the target. Taking bets on whether or not the prey would escape would be foolish. The situation is similar to matter crossing the event horizon of a black hole. There is no coming back from that.

There is no escape from the gravity of the situation. The inevitable capture by the black hole that is Gasolina is his final destiny. Pray that Gasolina's gravity never captures you.

Gasolina had her next meal. She would be his. Surprisingly, Gasolina found herself thinking about him. Most of the time, she didn't even imagine sexual relations when they made her dance erotically. It did nothing for her. What was turning on others was simply her work. It was nothing more than that. Now, finally. Now, she had feelings. What seemed before to be a game that she had to play in order to get a man. This time was different. There was moistness developing on the inner layer of her powder blue silk panties.

"Shit! I'll have smegma now." She said, rapidly changing her panties.

The new panties were a shimmering satin. She installed a thin pantyliner into the new pair. In case she got the opportunity, the liner was easy to discard, and the scent was pleasant. If he got up the nerve tonight. Hopefully, it will be this night. Tomorrow her period would come, with all the bloody nastiness that entails. Even if she could get away with hiding her heavy flow with a super-sized tampon. She would not be able to have that odor covered up merely by a scented pantyliner. She would have a heavy-duty smell pouring out of her. As her body ejected an old egg and the outer layer of skin from the inner layer of her lady cave.

"Today must be the day," Gasolina said to herself.

She wasn't getting any younger. Tonight catching her man was the most important thing on her mind. With that thought, she broke out the case containing her most expensive and best make-up collection. She couldn't leave anything to chance. Tonight the illuminated and practically fluorescent Gasolina would be the star.

She would capture her prey and feast on the wealth of his entire soul. When Gasolina set her mind to a task, she wouldn't stop until the job was completed. Her job at hand was the capture and domestication of that man. She didn't even know his name, but she knew that tonight he would return. If he knew of her plans and what was in store for his future, the next move he would be making was a u-turn. He missed all the signs telling him to turn back. Go home and find something else to do with his time. Collating files on his computer and rubbing one out, then drinking a beer before falling asleep. Watching TV would have been the best course of action. It is rare for a bachelor to follow the best course of action. He was not any different from those men that had come before him.

In the case of Gasolina, so many had come before him. He was not ignorant of this fact. His lust, the lust that he held so deeply in his heart, was out of control. The craving was running his life. She would become his. Her spell was cast. She could be a toothless sea-hag, and still, she would be the one for him.

She was good at her craft. Those skills were handed down to her. According to her mother, her great-grandma went to considerable lengths to ensure her grandma would learn the craft. Even though her grandfather, a Baptist minister, had made such a fuss over how it was a work of Satan to cast a spell. Any spell at all, even harmless ones.

The majority of the family spells that her great grandmother was the caretaker of were lost. Grandpa burned all the books that belonged to her. It's almost inevitable that Gasolina would not be working as an erotic, exotic dancer if those family spells of wealth, love, and power survived.

The spells and hexes didn't survive, but Gasolina was still a magical and spiritually active girl. Her attempts to deliberately capture the heart of the men she had in her life had always come to some success. However, there was a twist. Some strange bit of nonsense crept into these relationships. That had some bit of magic at the foundation of them. None of them lasted for any length of time.

Relationships brought together by magic don't generally stay together after the spell wears off. Awareness of this magical limitation stopped her from casting any spell this time. The romantic disasters from her active sexual past were a reminder, pointing out what may happen if she were to let the temptation overcome her. That was intellectual knowledge of what may come of a botched spell of love.

Joey, the taxidermist, her first love spell error had never recovered. The bacterial infection that consumed his manhood was her magic's side effect. She hadn't known about his suicidal tendencies. After the rotting of his penis into a putrid mess of untreatable goo, his suicide was almost entirely understandable. She had loved Joey. Although it was not something she would admit.

His mother had organized joey's funeral. She insisted he be buried with plenty of those disgusting furry creations of his. If archeologists ever disinter Joey's grave, they will be surprised to find his bones and the lifelike animals still looking fresh. It will surely give them quite a fright!

He, on the other hand, smelled fresh and alive. The energy

exuded from his pores, both excited and terrified her with power. She couldn't wait to be pressed into a clean sheet by his sweaty body. Unconsciously, her hand crept into the inside of her panties. The pantyliner was already a sticky mess. She caught herself diddling her clitoris and realized he must be the one for her.

Gasolina expected him soon. Her set was next. She was on after Sue, the lactating cow. What an ugly bitch she was. Who could have got hard enough to impregnate that heifer? Anyways, it doesn't matter. She would look like a fresh young princess compared to Sue. The tips would pour in as soon as she showed her marvelous tits.

Finally, Sue finished her desperate act of perspiration. Gasolina pranced out onto the main stage like an African gazelle, handing her a towel. Her eyes showed the crowd that, unlike a beast of prey, she was the predator. They all felt it inside their innermost brain, deep down in the lizard section, where the truly exciting thoughts dwell. Almost at an instinctual level, she locked her eyes with them. Each bar dweller felt her gaze and the warmth of her soul. Gasolina could make the whole crowd of unruly men feel as if they were alone with her entertaining them.

The DJ queued up the Edge of Seventeen by Stevie Nicks. He was being a little sarcastic with the song since the years back to seventeen were more than seventeen for Gasolina. She was the exotic dancer.

Then he announced, "Give it up for Sexy Sue! And now the immortal and ever-impressive Gasolina!"

The DJ would be spared a spiked heal to his metatarsal bones for the "immortal" quip, only because she wanted to be sweet in front of her man. She still didn't know his name. She had to remember to ask him. It would be unseemly of her to get a proposal before she even knew his name.

Clicking her heels together, the candy red six-inch pumps appeared to be the ruby red slippers of Dorothy. Unlike Dorothy, Gasolina had the personality of the witches. Whether that be Glenda the Good, or one of the bad witches depended utterly on the circumstances. The immortal Gasolina took to the stage.

1 2

The Black Telephone

Ecclesiastes 1:9 The thing that hath been, it is that which shall be; and that which is done is that which shall be done: and there is no new thing under the sun.

Laqueesha didn't know what to do. Scott had flirted constantly with her over the course of the last few weeks. She had seen the pictures of his dick. She knew he was horny for her and that he wanted to be doing the fucking. Laqueesha understood the functionality of that process. She completely understood it. Her mother had explained it. It would hurt at first, and then it would be fine. Always put a condom on it, unless you want to have a baby, and she remembered the words. "Baby, you are still a baby, don't have a baby." They rang in her ears as she remembered there was no condom.

"Scott, I forgot the condom." She said.

This was the first time they had been alone enough to get this far along the love-making process. Her mother was at work, and Tyrone was downstairs playing video games. He had the headphones on and wouldn't hear a thing. Even if he did, he wouldn't give a shit. He didn't care about her at all.

Scott was the first real man that Laqueesha had met. He was tall. He was handsome. He had a great mustache and the smile. Wow, his smile sparkled with the one gold tooth in front shimmering in the light that flickered in through the open window. It was strange she was now thinking about that light and the buzz it always made.

"Why do lights buzz?" She asked herself, stupidly straying off of the topic at hand, which was sex.

She had promised not to lose her virginity. Promises like that are empty promises because things happen and times come. Only God knows the right time. This time, however, didn't feel right to Laqueesha anymore. The fear was building up inside her, and her lips trembled as Scott touched her firm breasts. It all felt wrong. Suddenly she didn't want to be there anymore. She didn't want to be in her home. She didn't want Scott there trying to fuck around and take her virginity without a condom. Why was it her responsibility to have a condom? Where could she get one?

"This is just so much shit." She thought to herself.

Being 35 years old, Scott had access to resources beyond Laqueesha's ability to imagine. His homely wife never put out anymore, and he needed to get laid. This chick was hot. Super hot with her tight little butt inside of the Levi cutoffs. Her big knobby nipples stuck out of her braless t-shirt. His dick was so hard now. It had to have some pun tang now. The fucking little bitch was crying.

"What the fuck, Laqueesha? We talked about this. Don't worry. It won't hurt. It will be fun. You're going to love it. All the chicks love it when I fuckem'" Scott said, unzipping his pants to reveal yellow sponge bob boxer shorts.

He took her hand and placed it on his dick. She could feel it hard and throbbing under Patrick's face. Tears started to run down her beautiful brown cheeks. Her head started to shake no.

"I don't want to do this anymore, Scott. Can't we go downstairs and play video games with Tyrone? Maybe next week, when we have a condom, we can try it. I am so scared."

She wasn't a pretty sight anymore. The snot was dripping out of her nostrils, mixing with the tears and making a sticky paste of mucus. She could taste it at the corner of her mouth. It made her sick, and her stomach started to rumble. The rumbling, awful feeling that comes just before you spew. Yep, she was going to barf, and it was going to go all over Scott. He wasn't helping at all. He was grossing her out by licking the snotty mucus from her face.

"Queesha, relax. It will be okay," he said as he cleaned her tears and snot off of her upper lip and cheek.

She couldn't hold it in anymore. She barfed. All the Chucky Cheezy Pizza came out. All of it, over his face, some of it into his mouth.

"Ahgh!, You bitch!" Scott said, punching her hard.

Laqueesha saw stars. She fell down; off of the sofa, and her head hit the side of the radiator. It's super hotness searing into her forehead. The scream she emitted was piercing. Tyrone could hear it through the sound of machine guns and rockets. It cut through his noise-dampening headphones.

"Thefuck?" He said and took the phones off, and then clearly, he could hear his sister whimpering above his head.

He set the controller down and raced up the stairs. When he got to the top, he was confronted with Scott's big black naked butt. His dick was in his hand. The Spongebob shorts were hanging down between his knees. His sister lay on the floor. Laqueesha whimpered. Holding her head in one hand and her other hand under her body, covering her crotch. Her panties were pulled down. It looked bad. Scott was turning out to be a real prick.

Tyrone reached for the first thing he could find. It was a telephone. Big, black, heavy, and hard. The old phone hadn't been used in years. Everyone has smartphones these days. That black phone had a use still. It fit perfectly in Tyrone's hand. He picked it up and brought it down hard on the back of Scott's nappy head. He wasn't thinking anymore. He brought the phone down again and again. Blood filled the room. Scott fell, landing right on top of Laqueesha. The force of the fall finally pushed her face off of the hot radiator to her relief.

Laqueesha pulled herself out from under Scott, turned around, and looked at the mess. Scott lay there, with his boxers around his knees and obvious dents in his skull from the telephone. The phone had proven to be stronger than Scott's skull. Tyrone had done a real good job of making sure that Scott was going to remain dead. He lay there with his naked butt up in the air. It was awful. It was grotesque. Tyrone and Laqueesha looked at each other for some strange reason and smiled, breaking out into laughter. They were laughing over the body of Laqueesha's almost rapist boyfriend.

Laqueesha pulled up her panties, and just as she got them up. Before she could even adjust them, Tyrone disappeared. It was only for a moment as he reappeared in front of her. They were both floating above the house they had called home. Then there was light. They couldn't see anything. It was so bright, and they couldn't move.

The beam of light pulled them rapidly up and away from home. In moments, they were inside a dark room. There was a loud resonating voice that was repeating the words. "Remove your clothing for purification."

"I'm not getting naked in front of him!" Laqueesha yelled.

She was not getting how stupid that was since he had recently seen her exposed genitals in the upstairs room.

Tyrone was getting it. This was the most vivid dream he'd ever had. Removing his shirt at the second request, socks, pants, shorts followed shortly. He stood there naked. His sister finally followed his example and did the same. It wasn't the first time they'd been naked around each other. The shock and recent terrifying situation had Laqueesha on the defensive. The purification process began.

Purification was actually cleaning. All the exterior bacteria and parasites had to be removed from the twins. It tingled, and both of them felt embarrassed when Tyrone became erect. His sperm flew into the air right after. It disappeared before hitting the ground. His erection disappeared soon afterward.

"You are so gross, Tyrone," Laqueesha said, giggling and pointing.

She stopped laughing as her body lost control as well. Her bowels evacuated as she was completely cleaned.

They both stood empty in front of each other. In a matter of moments, they had gone from an attempted rape and killing scene to join some sort of sick pee pee, poo poo sci-fi movie. This was so strange to her, Laqueesha began to cry.

13

Transition Officer Gwendolyn

"This is weird. Tyrone, I wanna go home."

Tyrone didn't know what to do about it. He couldn't tell that to Laqueesha. She was shaking and naked. He was now a murderer. He had killed Laqueesha's boyfriend. It had happened suddenly. Without thinking, Tyrone had smashed a man's brains out. His sister had been there. She was about to be raped by her boyfriend. He had acted without thinking. Was it murder? Would he go to jail? Tyrone didn't know, and it scared him. Whatever happened, he didn't want his sister to see him scared.

"We've got to get out of here, sis," Tyrone said, looking for a door.

No door was visible in the room. It was lit dimly, and the light source was not visible. The room glowed. Any direction you looked, there was enough light to see, and that was all the light there was. There was enough light to see Laqueesha standing naked in front of him.

It wasn't the first time he had seen her birthday suit. They had grown up together. It was the first time he had seen her while his penis was hard. He wasn't thinking about her sexually. The purification process left him in this state. Recently, Tyrone had learned how good it felt to touch his penis. He could make it spit out if he thought about girls. His dreams were filled with girls. Naked girls, clothed girls, any girl except for Laqueesha. Now here he stood, and she was whimpering standing in front of him. She looked up at him, catching his eye. She stopped crying. Then pointed at his cock and started to laugh. That did it for him. The embarrassment caused his erect member to deflate like a popped balloon. He laughed too, as a fine mist filled the room. Suddenly, their predicament had become hysterical. The foggy gas had a euphoric effect on them. The powerful impact didn't last long, and they became sleepy. Both of them lost balance at the same time and hit the floor. The fall made them burst out laughing all the more. They hugged each other and fell asleep. Things were about to get real, and reality was more than their 13-year-old minds could ever have imagined.

Tyrone woke up. He didn't move a muscle. His eyes barely opened. He knew he wasn't home, and saving his sister hadn't been a dream. This was reality, and he was confused. It was pretty cool, though.

He lay in a bunk. It was the most comfortable bed he could have ever imagined. This beat the stinky foam pad he called a bed at home. His body was snug, fitted, and consumed by a form-fitting mattress. It wasn't that wide, but it was comfortable. There was a wall to his left, and to the right was another bunk, and he could see Laqueesha's head poking out of the blanket. All of her hair was missing. She lay there sleeping with her head resting on a white pillow. She had a bit of drool running down her chin. Her snores were like a shifting motorbike. Obviously, she was enjoying the bed in her dreams. Tyrone used the alone time to collect his thoughts.

He was in a room with no doors. He couldn't judge the dimensions of the room from his vantage point. The grayish-white wall next to him was firm, the one next to Laqueesha as well. She was two yards to the right. Her bunk was next to a visible wall. The problem was he couldn't see the other two walls. The floor and the ceiling weren't visible either. His bunk was firmly against a wall. He looked across at his sister's bunk. It was black with a thin silky blue blanket stretched tightly over her. He saw all of her body's curves and dents through it. Her forehead didn't have any marks on it. The burn marks were gone. They had been there before they fell asleep laughing, so they must have been in bed for quite a long time.

Laqueesha stirred a bit, sneezing. The blast sent some snot flying onto the clean blanket. She didn't seem to notice. She scratched her butt and then her eyes before opening them. Her hands went to her face. She noticed the drool, wiping it on a corner of her silky blanket. Then she touched her forehead.

"Oh, I thought I hurt myself last night. My God! Scott was going to rape me. Tyrone, you saved me. I owe you, bro. Just let me know. I will do anything for you. You're the best brother a sister could ever have. I love you, Tyrone," Laqueesha said with a seriously wide-eyed look that seemed to stare straight through Tyrone's brain.

Maybe he had done the right thing. He was always screwing up, but he had saved his sister this time, and that's a good thing. He did a good thing.

It was then that the wall, which wasn't quite visible, opened, and in walked a dream girl. Someone right out of one of his most secret dreams. She was tall, at least 5'10", with long curly blond hair that fell over her outfit and reminded him of a UFO rerun. The shimmery silver cloth clung to her figure. Big perky nipples swelled through the thin material. The pink was covered, yet he could still see the pink. It was so shimmery and see-through. Her skirt covered her panties, barely. He could tell she was wearing panties because they were visible through the skirt. She had on boots. Tyrone realized she wasn't 5'10" because the shiny black boots she wore had big heals on them. She was too much of a sight for him to take in this early morning, and his dick began to swell. His hands went down to his crotch and covered it up.

The lady said, "Good morning, children," while looking straight into Tyrone's eyes, smiling.

"I'm sure you have many questions. The past few hours must have confused you. Don't worry. I understand completely how you must feel. It is difficult to be plucked out of your surroundings and thrown into a strange situation in the blink of an eye. What you just went through, I have experienced as well.

My name is Gwendolyn, and I will be your transition officer. You are about to enter a new world that you could never have imagined. I'll be here for you to make sure you are safely processed. You will be adequately prepared for the reality you will experience.

Tyrone, don't be shy. Your body is behaving properly. What you are feeling is due to the purification process. Some of the chemicals used have that effect on men. Nobody will fault you or make fun of you because of it. Everyone has experienced that. It is likely nobody will even notice."

She turned and bent over Laqueesha's bunk after she finished her introduction. She touched her forehead, inspecting Laqueesha's face. Looking for damage, and all the while, she was cooing like a pigeon.

Tyrone was sure he had fallen in love and stared without blinking at Gwendolyn's hips. She was so perfect to his juvenile eyes. He had never been this close to such a beautiful woman, and she had even talked to him.

"Your forehead is completely healed, Laqueesha. I know you were worried there would be a burn scar. The purification process has healed all your wounds. It removed all visible scars from your body. You are as good as new. You're going to grow up to be a beautiful woman."

Laqueesha smiled, and her big eyes beamed happiness. She was looking straight into the eyes of their appointed transition officer. Whatever transition officer meant didn't matter right now.

Tyrone knew by the look in Laqueesha's eyes that his sister was going to be okay, and his erection finally deflated, leaving a small wet stain on the blanket. He could tell things would be alright, and he wasn't going to Juvenile Hall for killing Scott.

" Well, don't lay down all day. Get out of bed and come with me. It's time for breakfast, and I'm sure you're famished." Gwendolyn said.

Tyrone and Laqueesha didn't waste a second at the thought of breakfast and jumped out of bed. Then they realized they were completely naked.

"Don't worry about your clothing. We'll get you some uniforms along the way to the dining facility. Follow me!" She made a quick about-face like an ROTC cadet and walked towards the magically appearing door. The kids quickly got in line and walked out that magical door.

14

Take Me Home

Gasolina tripped. It was an explosive move, and she fell hard. Her broken high heel flew away. Gasolina fell off the stage and into the man's lap. She had successfully completed the maneuver. Ground control had not seen it coming. Whump! Her rump went thump on her man's lump. What a chump. She smiled and giggled. "Wheee!"

The man was startled. He spilled his drink all over the pretty dancer. Her glitter shimmered as the amber liquid of his bourbon and beer dripped off of her breasts.

"Don't just stare. Wipe me off, sweetheart. This lap dance is on the house!" As Gasolina encircled the man's head with her wrists, forcing his head between her lovely wet breasts.

He didn't know what to do. He couldn't reach the napkin. His glasses were covered with sweat, bourbon, and some concoction of shimmering glitter and coconut oil. His already semi-erect dick sprang to full attention, and he submitted to the inevitable messy conclusion.

"This isn't so bad." He thought to himself. She said it was on the house, and he was already fully aroused.

He couldn't resist taking one of her nipples between his lips. He gave it a playful tug which resulted in another "Reeee" from the delighted Gasolina.

Gasolina felt the warmth and knew the man's pants would be stained from this slip of fate. There was nothing to worry about. It felt good, and she wanted more. He could give her more. This handsome young man would drive her mad and treat her like the naughty girl she was. It wouldn't wait. It was going to happen tonight! She reached down between her legs and put her hand on his moist crotch. She could feel his soul throbbing through the pants. She put her fingers up to her nose and inhaled his scent. Her nostrils fluttered, and she shuddered. He had an intensely fragrant aroma. She sniffed again and rubbed it in her hair. Then she forced her panties down on the mess and rubbed herself to a quick little happy place. She glowed and smiled ear to ear.

The man was so enthralled with the fast turn of the events. He had just sat at the stage with his drink. He looked up as the gas giant Gasolina had landed in his lap. Now he was a mess, and his face turned red. The embarrassment of the moment was setting in. His pants were covered in sperm, and his face was covered with glitter. This was his last lap dance of the night.

"Well," he thought. "At least it was her; she is my fantasy girl."

"Take me home, big guy. I want to feel you inside me tonight. I'm going to change my clothes. Wait for me." Gasolina whispered in his ear.

She walked barefoot with her heels held high above her head, her breasts bouncing, and her high-pitched voice giggling, "out of my way."

The car's engine roared. Gasolina looked at the dash. The bench seat was nice, and the rear seats looked roomy, actually huge. What a beautiful 2-door Pontiac. The blue was as deep as the man's eyes. The engine's vibration was spectacular. They rolled down the highway towards her home. She thought about leaning over and giving him head on the highway. She had done it before, but she didn't want him to think of her as a slut. He seemed embarrassed still about the wet stain on the front of his pants. No worries, he was almost hers. She would fully seal the deal tonight. She could feel it was alright.

So many rhymes filled her head as she thought about the happiness for her and her family to come. He wasn't dumb, but he would be controllable; he was young. She could direct him and raise him to be the husband she needed, and it pleased her to believe he would be happy with her. She could give him the attention he craved.

He weaved suddenly in the road as a flash of light lit the night like lightning cutting through the dark. Except it remained illuminated. More than the flash of time expected from a lightning strike. He regained control of the car. The land yacht continued its roaring voyage towards Gasolina's home port.

"What was that Hon," She said.

He shook his head. He didn't have any idea, but it was gone. He wasn't going to worry about it tonight. He was thinking happy thoughts of what would happen next. She had all but told him they would be fucking tonight. He couldn't imagine it would move so fast. He was so lucky today. Everything was going to be okay.

The rest of the ride was smooth. The man was getting playful as she fumbled for the keys and gave him a shhh with her finger so as not to wake up the kids. She put his arms over his shoulders and embraced his firm upper body. He followed the lead with his arms around her waist, and in no time, his hands cupped her buns firmly. They kissed.

It was their first kiss. Slow, warm, soft, and passionate, wow, he knew how to kiss. Gasolina's shivered and pushed her hips forward into his embrace. She could feel him becoming aroused again, and it felt right. This was right. He would be the man to solve her problems, and the kids would love him.

"Let's go upstairs," Gasolina whispered. Quietly pointing to the ceiling, they worked their way to the stairs.

Like a couple of kids in a sack race, they wouldn't let go of the embrace. It was to good. After a bit of nonverbal negotiations, they finally got to the top of the stairs.

She was proud of her two-bedroom, two-bath duplex. At least she had something to show for her hard work, and the mortgage wasn't that bad. In a few more years, it would be hers, and she would have a place to live when she retired, unlike some of her friends, that never planned ahead. Now they hang around bars giving head to pay for their beer. Their beat-up trailers were full of their good-for-nothing kids. Her kids were in the magnet school and doing great. Gasolina had a lot to be proud of.

The man let go over her and was standing, staring. His jaw opened up, and he pointed his hand behind her. Something didn't look right with the expression on his face. It was changing from intense desire to obvious terror.

She turned around and then, at the top of her lungs, screamed! "Oh Jesus! Oh, God! What happened? Where are my babies? Oh God, Oh God. Oh God, help me!"

Tears and terror filled the face of Gasolina as she looked at the naked butt of Laqueesha's boyfriend. His pants and Spongebob shorts were down around his knees. His head was broken and bloody. A puddle of fresh red blood on the white tile of Laqueesha and Tyrone's bedroom floor. The man pulled himself together, rapidly embracing the woman. He brought her close to him again, covering her face with his big hand.

There was no sign of Tyrone or Laqueesha. The phone beeping beep, beep, beep laying on the floor covered in blood left no clue into how Scott had died. Gasolina had an idea but kept her mouth shut to it as the man held her tight. He wasn't letting go. This man is a good man, Gasolina thought. "Thank you God, for bringing him to me." She let out a prayer. "Oh Father God, the master of the heavens and earth. Please God, help me find my children. Oh God, I don't know what happened. Help me make it okay. In Jesus's name, amen."

The man followed with an "Amen."

She didn't know what to do, but she knew from the sound of that Amen things would be okay.

***

I will save my aggression for a spell, and if that time never comes, die peacefully and happily without regrets. My mighty pen is losing ink fast. Time to load the converter or switch over to my Otto Proud. There's dark blue ink in the cartridge. I thought it was black until I saw it in the Incandescent light. I'm getting tired of having my colors removed by these LED lights. This ink is fine. Blue is a way to celebrate into the dark void. That is our final destination.

Just a time, and then we join a clutter of space noise and an unbroken stream of the dead. Our deathly consciousnesses all connected, streaming and twisting through the Milky Way Galaxy. This is the total of the collective consciousness of ourselves and our ancestors, not to mention the endless clutter of our pets. Then there are those animals who have been our dinners' conscious screams. We are all connected, but some escape into the endless stream behind our planet Earth.

The blue ink earlier must have mixed with the black. Since I don't have an otto converter, I'm confident that the ink was also black from the cartridge. The ink dries so quickly I rarely smear it. As always, the iridium M nib short two electrons from gold. It's trying hard to please, forever unable to bend like its richer cousin with 79 electrons. It's a prime number, and the metal is bendy. Gold shines more than any other metal I know. Iridium does its best to please, and the price is right, so nobody ever complains about it. It isn't going to do the job today.

It's like a drug, being back on the black sailor ink. It lays the solder down, the way the ink pours out of the nib. The black, sticky ink catches souls and spits them out onto the pages. These people won't know what hit them. The story continues with my wonderful Aurora pen advancing the plot. It is thick with the proper bounce to the 14-carat gold nib. There is a zen feeling to it. So graceful and relaxing that I lose my aggressive thoughts and feelings; they become lost in space between the lines. Ruled paper is forcing me to follow the rules. There is a lull in the violence, and our cast takes a time out for lunch.

15

Professor Dick

The field is the sole governing agency of matter. ~ Albert Einstein

The brainwaves of one person may interact with the brain-waves of another. This is a provable electromagnetic interaction.

As we stand in the present, our body and consciousness should live on top of our written history. This foundation we stand on has a significant control over where we will end up in our unlimited potential futures. Our consciousness exists in all of these unlimited futures. We only perceive the present. We can't see the future. You, as an individual, actually have glorious happenings in the future.

The angels of God see these potential futures. That place you find yourself in may not be the future the angels saw, if you turned left instead of right. They gave you a nudge towards the right. You ignored it and are sitting into a puddle of mud from your lack of sensitivity to your environment.

You were riding your bike down the road and felt a sudden compelling reason to turn to the right. For some reason, you turned to the left. You saw the mud puddle. You knew what would happen, and you still rode into the puddle on the left. That little soft voice telling you to turn right slips from memory rapidly. You sit bruised, wet and upset in a cold puddle of mud. This is only one way the event happened. There exists another reality where you listened to the soft voice of the angel and steered right. This alternate future is equally valid. You are riding down the road, feeling fabulous with a grin above your chin. You listened to a quiet, strange voice tell you to.

"Stay on the right, and keep your eyes forward."

You are in both of these places. You experience both of these realities as "reality." Your conscious thoughts have split and branched off into another universe. This universe-splitting event happens in an imperceptible instant. You begin to exist in another universe, a universe where you have a shared history. Your present circumstances are entirely different from the puddle of mud universe. There is a new future in store for you riding down the road with that smile on your face. You exist simultaneously in both universes. There are more than these two paths that share your consciousness. There are an unlimited number of potential universes, and your destiny exists in them. Each of these universes is equally valid. Each of these universes includes your history. These universes begin new at every intersection of reality.

It is hard to get moving on the path the angels set for you. That is because they don't set a course. Angels only help influence the outcomes of events to ensure the most optimum result. For both you and the rest of the universes that are influenced by your actions. You have many possible moves. The best move that benefits reality the most will always be encouraged by the angels. Our futures are built based on the actions we take.

***

Even though it seems like a planet, ROM is something more and something less all at once. It is a place that encompasses all locations, yet is nowhere. ROM is where you are when you see what is happening but cannot affect the outcome of that which is observed. The etymological roots are in an acronym from the late 20th century, which stood for Read Only Mode. When in ROM, all time-space has the possibility of observation. Interference is limited. It is almost impossible to interfere. Fortunately almost doesn't count for much these days. Since if it is possible, it will happen. Even the improbable happens infinitely many times in an open infinite universe.

Tyrone was daydreaming. The class was boring. Sure it was necessary to learn about ROM, but why be so technical? The engineering of ROM was impossibly complicated. He would never be on the engineering staff.

His thoughts turned towards Gwendolyn again. Her perfect form was always on his mind. The slinky pantsuit she wore today was especially troubling. The legs sliced up the sides, revealing her shapely legs. When she stepped off, the curves were visible all the way up to her hips. Gwendolyn's naked hip, the thought of her hips made Tyrone squirm in the chair, trying to find a less conspicuous position that wouldn't reveal his engorged cock. It had a mind of its own. There was Tyrone, and there was his cock. Both of them connected to the same body and stuck in the same lecture about ROM. Dick, the holographic instructor, didn't care about Tyrone's teenage predicament. He continued to drone on about ROM.

"The primary focus of ROM's mission is observation. Careful observations made of multiple field views of the ever-evolving worlds, encompass Earth's multi-world view. The alternate paths and outcomes of these trajectories are carefully analyzed in order, to prevent major synchronized catastrophic events over multiple Earths. It is sometimes easier to understand this by viewing diagrams. Here is a diagram showing the path of the Earth through space-time. This diagram simplifies the actual multiple paths that are tracked 8-dimensionally by ROM. Each branch of the diagram represents an alternate reality for the planet Earth. Where these branches reconnect at the vertices, major events are tracked. We enter the world of our ancestors' gods. When these vertices and rows are mapped into eight dimensions." The professor droned on and on.

Dick wasn't really a dick. He was rather good at drawing diagrams. His soul's essence had been captured, but he had refused to accept the transfer to a new body. His ability to explain the incomprehensible was unmatched. He had agreed to take a holographic form to help newly arrived residents of ROM. The recently arrived, needed to understand what their actual position in the universe was.

"Tyrone! You're permanently gross." Laqueesha said when she noticed what he was trying to cover up.

"This is important; pay attention. The only dick you should be concentrating on is Professor Dick." She said, pointing with her lips to the holograph and the diagram.

Dick noticed the small commotion. He rather liked these two kids. The youngest fully recovered members of ROM were intelligent, handsome, and from what he knew of events, their bravery would be important for some moments in space-time. Still, they were kids, and he had to get their attention.

"Tyrone, can you explain what happens when the lines of the diagram intersect?" Dick said, calling on the tall teenage boy.

"Professor Dick, that's like my mother used to call an event. It's a cusp. Where things come together, that's where the magic happens." Tyrone said.

His thoughts turned away from Gwendolyn long enough to answer the question. The question brought up memories of his mother. He worried about her, now that Laqueesha and himself were gone. What would she do? Her life must be a turmoil after the way they left, vanishing into nothing and leaving a dead, half-naked man in the house. It must have caused her massive heartache. He imagined that the police would have come, and the TV news and how embarrassed his mom would have been.

Her profession was not discussed at home, but he knew she was a stripper. He knew she danced naked for men to see. He knew she did it for Laqueesha and him so that they could have a decent life. He imagined the headlines in the paper.

"Stripper Prime Suspect in Death of Married Man," or some other shit like that. They wouldn't be kind to his mother, and now he was getting angry.

"What is up with this emotional roller coaster I'm riding these days?" Tyrone said to himself.

Dick heard it. He heard everything that happened in his classroom. Being a holographic entity had its benefits.

"You're turning into a man, son. The chemical interactions inside your body are changing. It disrupts you in unpredictable ways. The only thing predictable about it, is that it happens to all of us over time." Dick said, sympathetic to the boy's dilemma.

Growing up was tough enough, and being in an alien environment made it that much tougher. Tyrone would have a lot to overcome, and getting a grasp of ROM was imperative to his role aboard her.

Dick thought of ROM as a woman. She wasn't a ship, but she was a ship in his mind. They were sailing a course across the universe towards a distant unseen goal. The tempest that always seemed to find its way into their course was to be out-flanked. The peaceful times between were his favorite times. Teaching these two youngsters was his primary goal now. He would make them the best possible agents for change in this crazy mixed-up world of a machine they lived in.

"That's a good analogy, Tyrone, but it isn't exactly correct. It's not so much a cusp as an intersection of hyper-dimensional polygons. We look for what occurs inside the volume of these intersections. That's our focus, and it's where the magic really happens. The volume in-between the intersection of hyper polygonal shapes that represent the Earth's many-worlds is where the events happen. These alignments of neighbors give ROM the ability to step outside of read-only mode. These momentary alignments allow for effective changes. Transfiguring the course and outcome of reality.

For example these intersections are where ROM agents like yourselves are relocated to our crew complement. We see the probable outcomes of such events. Then determine if your continued existence will be of significant importance on the current probabilistic trajectory your world is making. If it is found that you could be of use to the ROM. Your removal proves to be insignificant to the course of Earth. Then we capture you. Adding you to the roster of our crew. Of course, many other actions or inactions are available to us. Inside of these intersections, the outcomes are predicable and probable, but not guaranteed. As far as being a cusp, no it's not a cusp. The lines are sharp. The potentials are certainly potential. Potential clear lines of probability are moving towards multiple predicted outcomes. Compute the eigenvector, and plot the vertices. The parabola of the cusps and their measured curves are important inside the volume of intersections..." Dick droned on.

Tyrone got the gist of it. The math made him sleepy. They worried about things that happened inside intersections. When the light turns red, or green what happens to the people inside the cars. It didn't matter what happened in the curves...

He dozed off again into a dream. Gwendolyn was there and they were at the beach. The white sandy spit that stuck out near Forever Falls. The recreation area he was familiar with here in ROM.

She wore a red two-piece bikini. It was sort of two piece and a little bit like a bikini. It was red yarn with triangles attached in three strategic locations. The intersection of these vertices had Tyrone's primary focus. The probability of entering the volume of this intersection was highly improbable. Over the course of the lifetime of the universe even improbabilities happened. Infinite amounts of time, he smiled, and realized he was starting to get it. This Dick was getting through his thick skull. Ugh, he was thinking about Dick again, and the sweet dream of paradise evaporated away.

Tyrone snorted back to the awakened world. Professor Dick asked him another question. "Why are we selected to join the ROM's crew?"

Tyrone replied, he was finally getting it. "Because we are insignificant. We don't matter to the world. We are worthless, so it doesn't matter if we disappear never to return. Nobody will miss us anyway."

Dick was saddened by this. Tyrone and his sister Laqueesha were important. Perhaps the most important people Dick had ever met. He had met some powerful people over the course of his existence. Tyrone was young and didn't get it. His role in effecting the probable outcome of events to come was important. He was not insignificant, he had a purpose.

"You are not quite getting it Tyrone. You are on the right track, but in the wrong position. ROM determined that your role in the universe would be more significant if you joined her crew. Onboard ROM you are not worthless. You've never been involved in an operation, so you don't have a mental picture of how you will effect reality. At least the reality that ROM is in." Dick said, trying to raise Tyrone's self-esteem up a peg.

Tyrone was frustrated, and finally the class ended. "Time to eat!" He screamed and ran out the door.

Dick smiled, closed his presentation, and hit the virtual switch labeled Power Nap. He'd take a quick trip to visit virtual Arline in heaven.

16

Bye Bye San Louis Obisbo

Pay attention to the dog licking your face and get up out of bed. Walk that dog instead of ignoring him. Don't roll over and catch an additional twenty minutes of sleep. That is taking action to move towards an optimum future with a walked dog. The less than best future is equally valid. You sleep the extra twenty minutes. Upon rolling out of bed, you promptly step into a new universe along with a pile of dog poop. Welcome to another reality. Learn your lesson with the dog poop, and start listening to the voices before you step in front of a moving car: before you walk under a ladder and have a paint can be dropped on your head. These realities will exist, but you won't step in the dog poop if you walk the dog.

Learn to listen to those voices. Dodge the car effectively. Then you may continue your existence in the current reality you inhabit. The alternates of that event could include futures that have a minor role in, except as landfill. There may be a worse future that includes you living. The car driver is dead from the car crash you caused by stepping in front of him. That universe exists, but if you are not experiencing it. Don't go out of your way to bring that reality to your current situation. Walk your dog and take a nap later.

Monkey, monkey, monkey. In India, they make homes and communities on the high walls of the larger cities like Madras. The monkeys use the humans in these cities. They harvest food from them. They stay apart from the people, except when they're stealing their meals. The monkey steals from the humans and often gets the more excellent option from stealing than people.

Dogs are man's favorite pet. Dogs eat the scraps that humans leave behind. They hang out in camps and provide some protection from wolves, the animal they descended from.

Monkeys have descended from the same ancestor of man. Millions of years ago, our ancestors took divergent paths. They didn't like each other then. They certainly don't like each other now.

Monkeys build communities next to humans since humans are the source of the monkey's food in most Asian nations. Unlike the dog, they remain wild and not domesticated. Their communities thrive among people, even where the human settlements lack or even starve. The monkey is not the human's slave. The monkey communities connected to them thrive or at least survive. The monkey is resilient. The monkey has been on a fantastically successful run as a species, essentially unchanged for millions of years.

Whereas dogs are entirely dependent on humans. Although feral dogs set up communities too. There's no resemblance between a dog community or a monkey's community. Canine towns of wild dogs have no resemblance to wolf packs, either. When left to their own, dog communities don't resemble that of the wolf, a nomadic animal.

Wolf packs move about in the wild. They never call one place home. Dogs will set up headquarters and build on that community. I am not talking about the African wild dog. That dog has been wild since their domesticated brethren left their new home of Africa and returned to Asia with their humans approximately thirty-thousand years ago. The DNA of these animals shows a relationship through the mitochondrial DNA investigation. Their 78 chromosomes are the same. They can breed among each other. They don't have anything in common with the solutions modern canines have arrived at. These feral dog communities are a European and North American phenomenon.

***

"That's 200," Henry said as he finished counting the ticks on the registry.

It had not always been this way. Henry, a trim, white 50-year-old man, had been born into an influential family in Dothan, Alabama. When he was young, his father had been a politician. He was on the city council. He'd even made an unsuccessful but lucrative attempt at running for governor. All the money from father was gone for 15 years now. If he had it, that money would not even buy a bicycle nowadays.

Henry closed the browser on the office computer with his company 200 Units less for the day. Mr. Chang would be happy with his work. It would be nice to visit his office again and get the opportunity to flirt with Clara Mae, his assistant. Henry was one of the lucky ones from Dothan. He had been in Birmingham at a party when the bomb had gone off. Dothan was a guarded, off-limits crater now. Pa, his brother Charles and Snackler, the black coon dog, were all gone in an instant. The fireball had consumed everything. China's fuel-air bomb technology worked well. Their strategic first strike had taken the entire world by surprise.

The US was not prepared. America had lost her ability to wage foreign war several years back. Budget cuts had forced the country to mothball its aircraft carriers and submarine fleet. The public welcomed the cost savings and the real estate sale of the naval bases to China for their import fleet to deliver goods. The public practically demanded it. They could not get enough of the goods that China was importing. Everyone had something from China; everything was from China.

American's chatting on social networks, and sitting on their Italian-style furniture designed in Milan and manufactured in the Philippines province of China, hardly noticed the war. China had selected its targets well. Inconsequential towns across America ceased to exist. No strategically essential assets of the US were affected. San Louis Obispo, California. Dothan, Alabama, Rapid City, South Dakota, Beckley, West Virginia were all important towns... to the residents. They were of little importance to the rest of the world. Only the government in Washington DC took notice. The Joint Chiefs of staff dutifully briefed the President on his retaliation options. The President then briefed congress on the options available to the United States. Congress debated the terms that China demanded.

China is a friendly nation. We are a nation of farmers and traders. The economic war your nation has fought with us has caused suffering beyond comprehension to a vast number of our citizenry. Our children have starved. Our families have been forced into involuntary separation. All because of your economic manipulation of the world's currency markets. Today the collective muscle of the Peoples Liberation Army has been felt across your country. Our targets were hit with precision and were well thought out to minimize collateral damage. The majority of your population was not affected and will not be unless our demands are not met...

Without a shot of anger being fired by the United States, the Sino American war was fought and won in a day by China. The final demilitarization of America began, and the

North American Union was born. Canada and Mexico had long since been puppets of the People's Republic of China. They remained untouched by the day of fire China rained on the United States. They were eager to join the new union, meeting China's demands.

North American Units were tied to the RMB. Dollars were traded for the next two years at three to one. Stability was restored. President Wu's election was clean and fair. He had run for president unopposed. Only his name had been on the ballot. Still, a majority of voters from Yucatan to Nunavut voted and cheered.

Upon announcement of the results, President Michael Hunt resigned. His appointment as interim governor of Florida was short-lived. He did not have much of an opportunity to enjoy the spoils victory. Five days after his resignation and appointment as governor, Uncle Mike died from a massive brain aneurism. He was found on his throne in his pajamas by his butler.

His newest bride, Sandra, was devastated. Unable to deal with the press, she committed suicide the following day. Her body was found hanging in the closet of her bedroom. There was a full minute of silence across the country. This was the remembrance of the last President of the United States.

Henry didn't think about it much; Mr. Chang had him busy. The death of his Pa and Snackler were not thought of anymore. All he had time for was making Mr. Chang happy. Production was down at the factory. Mr. Chang's line was responsible for the majority of the profit for the company.

With the Brazilian empire's technology improving, it seemed like the erosion in market share would not stop. Beijing had sent Chang to prevent the decline. His skill as a manager was proven. His severe punishment methods were no longer acceptable in modern China, so he was a perfect match for their factory in Dallas. The tiny transmitters they manufactured for controlling nanobots could be shipped from Rio as quickly, just as easily as they could be shipped from Dallas. Very few Europeans complained about the minute differences in personality that resulted from the use of the inferior Brazilian product. Erectile disfunction was cured. The ability to control oneself in public was not considered a problem in Paris these days. It did not matter how many sales staff he caned. The market share continued to dwindle.

17

Let's Roll

Don't cry when your dog dies. They live full dog lives when you take care of them. Petting, walking, feeding, the dog has lived a happy life. They perceived their existence at a different speed. They have lived an entire life.

You are like an angel to dogs, showing them the right way to go, perceiving the future they will likely exist in. If they are not walked, that future will result in a poopy urine-soaked living room carpet. Don't worry; the good dog will try to hide it. They will feel guilt for a moment, and they will regret it if you punish them quickly after the incident.

You already know that future, and you can help the dog exist in a happier future. Simply walking your canine will affect his time and space positively. There is little doubt that walking your dog makes for a better future. On the sad occasion where walking your dog results in being struck by a car or some other unlikely calamity occurs, an angel is sure to warn you about that event.

Angels might not give you a strong warning. They might not warn you at all if the future you face is going to result in an entertaining act for them.

"Haha, the human stepped in poop." They fell in the ditch. "Hahaha!" Says the angel.

The human will be hit by the car. This case will result in a hard warning. You must be looking for these signs. Don't make the evening news if you want to live a prosperous long life. Angels will help you avoid these situations. You have to let them help. We can always hope for the best. Even in the worst of situations, the angels will help if you let them. The results may not be what you wanted, but you will follow the best path available to you if you listen to them.

Even dogs have angels. I am confident of this. I have met a dog angel while walking my dog in Vancouver. My dog was recovering from bad treatment. While being shipped to America, he spent a week in Turkey. On arrival, he was a mess. He couldn't tell me what happened, only whimpers, but not who did it to him. I could only guess what had happened. He was already scabbing over and improving but not quite showing the zest for life he had in the past.

He took his first pee against the nearest tree. Then sniffed a bit. We both looked up, and there was an older lady. She had appeared in the less than 5 seconds I had looked away. She was sitting there smoking a cigarette. That smoke was halfway finished. She must have been there before. She didn't just magically appear. She reached her hand down, and my golden lab walked up to her and put his nose into her hand. She looked into his eyes, and he sat, relaxed without fidgeting. This is not normal behavior for my rambunctious boy. Scratching his head with her fingernail and blowing out a giant billow of blue tobacco smoke, she smiled at me. I smiled back and said. "Good evening, ma'am."

The dog angel gave me a quick rundown. She told me his wounds were from a shotgun. She promised me he would heal completely and to change his food immediately. She smiled again.

I said. "Thank you, ma'am," and we went to finish our walk.

She wasn't there when we returned. She had vanished as silently as she had arrived. I am sure this was a dog angel. I hope to meet her again. This time I will have so many questions and things to say. It's not normal for me to lack words. It is almost as if the words were taken from me. She had spent those few minutes of nonverbal communication with my dog. It had been more critical for him than for me. The world had revolved around my dog for that brief moment. It had been his turn to get attention. His behavior has completely changed for the better since that day. The dog angel taught my lab the right path to follow, and his life will be a successful dog life because of it.

When you meet an angel, how do you know? What do you do? Angels do walk the Earth. They have been here since the dawn of time, checking, testing, building, rejecting. Being rejected by an angel is to be rejected by the Lord God. They are the messengers of God. We never know who we meet face to face. What is their back story? Have you ever helped a stranger? Gone out of your way to do something nice for someone that can't in anyway help you? Angels may test this way. Angelic beings may pretend to be men on Earth. Nobody knows their reasons or intentions for what they do.

Testing is my opinion. Everyone talks a good game. How they do the right thing and follow the golden rule, but the fact is most of those among us don't. We tend to be selfish, only looking after our carnal desires. This is the actual state of man. The carnal man, with his thoughts and dreams that only include himself. It is impossible to grow or get success past a basic nomadic lifestyle if you only think about yourself. I'm talking about those that can't think about tomorrow until tomorrow actually comes. Work as a team growing and increasing your productivity by communicating. Yield to the better idea or plan when necessary. Don't be stubborn and hold on to a failed idea. This is hubris, and arrogance brings about failure.

It's been years since the Pentagon and Twin towers were toppled. My youngest son was an infant then. He doesn't remember. I remember. It delayed me driving to work. Listening to the news on the radio, I couldn't believe what I was hearing. When I arrived at the office, I read the news on the Internet. I saw the image. There was a gif over and over again. It was intolerable, awful and I became angry, but there was no target for my aggression. So I swallowed it. Then I stopped watching replays. In fact, I find it difficult to watch graphic violence. It makes me feel violent. It leaves me feeling sad and depressed for the victims. I prefer romance, drama, and science fiction.

Years ago, when Mr. Beamer organized the assault on the cockpit, successfully resulting in crashing an airliner full of people into a Pennsylvania farm instead of a building, it showed me the truth that there are angels among us. Not the shiny gossamer-winged creatures from lead paint artistic dreams. I'm talking about real angels. Whether or not they are of God is out of my league to judge, but we may indeed call them godly. How much more can an angel be godly if a cow may be considered godly?

That person you just closed the elevator door on, May have been sent by God. The angel to impart critical knowledge for you, strengthening you, and showing you the right way to turn. Yet the doors closed, and you won't have another chance with the angel. There will be other times and future occasions. That particular opportunity has passed you by. Through a simple act of selfishness, you gained an extra 1 second in the elevator. The additional moment saved, let that potential life-changing opportunity pass over you. Perhaps a fortune was lost. You will never know.

One thing is certain, there are plenty of angels. There is a multitude of the heavenly host; A multitude is a whole bunch. They aren't all for you, but some are for you. Even though you may never meet them or know of them, they're there.

Mr. Beamer had the opportunity to talk to his loved one a last time. An angel must have helped him connect. It's tough to get a cellphone signal at an altitude, especially in a rural corner of Pennsylvania. There was an angel in that pin drop. The plane still crashed. In fact, Beamer and his unnamed crew of heroes were responsible for the crash. We can all agree landing the plane would have been a better outcome, but in that situation, it wasn't going to happen. Mr. Beamer got to talk and was able to get a message out about what was happening. They were able to save so many lives. The conflagration of jet fuel and the hefty weight of the Boeing airliner would have been a devastating blow to a building. The angels had it easy; Beamer and the crew did the hard work. The angels were there, helping them do the hard things, helping them with their alternate sacrifice. Wait a minute, back up, you didn't just say that, did you? Yeah, well I did and I mean it. Here's why! Those very angels have helped me more than one time. That has kept me alive multiple times that I should have been dead. Not just me, but maybe you are among the living because of them too? I'm not going to dwell on my personal brushes with death. None of them was anything heroic, and I don't want to take away from some real American heroes.

Fine, but you are still crazy. What about those other passengers, well, what about them? Tragedies happen all the time and their deaths were indeed tragic. It is extremely likely the way the rest of that morning went. That plane was on its way to cause some real terror as the timeline through that morning went tick-tock, tick-tock. The least awful thing to happen was for that plane to be forced down.

Angels must have been crying that day as they powered the plane into the ground. The timeline was out of time. The accounts are clear and people still think about them and cry. All through that morning, there were chances and opportunities to cancel or delay those flights, including Todd Beamer's. It didn't happen.

Regrettably, every opportunity that the angels brought up all morning was ignored. Multiple angels were left outside the elevator doors that morning as chances to cancel or ground the flights were passed by. I'm not blaming the people that ignored those angels. Normally we all have that kick yourself in the butt moment. I know I have more times than I can remember. Those heavenly multitude were working hard. Americans were doing what they do best, ignoring the signs and portends of doom. Todd Beamer and the unnamed men with him did the right thing, listening to their angels, they crashed that plane.

What happened on those other planes? The angels must have been working hard. Because that is what the heavenly host do. Maybe someone was trying to reason with the terrorists. There must have been a similar make up of passengers on the other planes. There must have been guys with their angels telling them to move. But it just didn't work. Maybe the teamwork wasn't there. Some person trying to calm things down just didn't. Or they calmed down the wrong person. Regardless, that didn't work and those buildings fell down. The pentagon got trashed and a lot of people died. The angels were working overtime to stop that. The humans were working hard to do their jobs. Get those planes in the air and whatnot. That is what people do, Americans especially. They do their best. The INS did their best too. So did the FBI. Let's not forget the giant bass drum that an angel must have been beating when the pilot in training had no interest in learning to land the plane. When bam come a wham come a bam that big bass drum was beaten. Those planes still crashed.

Even after they crashed those planes, all those first responders had angels talking to them. I have heard the interviews. Every year now it's discussed on most of the radio shows in September. Some of those responsible for not apprehending the terrorists admit to hearing the angels, after the fact. They know they messed up. The expression 20/20 hindsight is used in these situations, but they knew it was an angel talking to them. They knew it was a screwup.

Why can't we go backward in time? Time-traveling forward only is all we're able to conjure up with our current level of technological advancement. We can only theorize as to the possibility of traveling at relativistic speed. Many of us dream about doing it. Angels are limited in their abilities, without the ability to time travel to the past. The past an angel sees is fully written. It can't be edited like a video game. Real-life is for taking seriously.

18

Henry Pays Attention

There was a blinding light, and the world became black. Henry floated above the mess like a rag-doll. His bowels evacuated. Which added to the mess from his bladder that had already emptied its liquid. He was a mess inside and out. Unable to speak, he could only observe the wreckage of the raft and his companion's bodies. Oddly enough, he couldn't see his own corpse littered among the broken bodies of his fellow insurrectionists. Their attempt at blowing up the maglev trestle was a complete failure. The train just floated by. The passengers didn't notice the failed attempt on their lives. It was sinking into Lake Pend Oreille, disappearing with their dreams of a return to free America into a deep watery grave.

Henry's thoughts turned to his own destiny. He was floating fast away from the scene when everything went black. The brief period of sensory depravation was interrupted by the voice of an angel. "Remove your clothing and prepare for purification."

The clothing evaporated away as it landed on the floor. The flecks of turds fell free from his body. The soil disappeared just as fast. Nothingness consumed his articles of clothing. The purification process was arousing. Henry's pecker was fully engorged, which made him feel awful instead of happy. Seeing the bodies of his compatriots floating on the lake had shaken him, yet the purifying the angel had warned him to prepare for would not stop stimulating his entire body. It didn't take long for him to release his sperm into the air. This embarrassing seed also evaporated away before hitting the ground. The globs of gooey semen glowed in the bluish light as they shot out of his erect penis. They never hit the floor. The same magical process that had cleaned and purified the area of the turds must have cleaned up the spunk too.

Gwendolyn sat silently in a chair near Henry's bedside. Her hands were folded neatly in her lap. Her feet were off to the left, gently touching together under her bent knees. She was the epitome of grace and patience. Her gaze never left the newcomer. She knew it would only be a matter of moments before the eyes on his handsome face would slowly open. He began to stir. Gwendolyn's back straightened as she went into full attention mode. Her pulse quickened with mounting anticipation. As predicted, Henry's eyes opened gradually, fluttering intermittently. He soon realized he was flat on his back, his eyes trying to focus on what should have been a ceiling. Gwendolyn spoke softly. "Hello and welcome Henry"

He rolled his head in her direction. He was in a hazy and confused state of mind, yet still recognized her exceptional beauty.

"Where am I?"

Henry tried to sit up, but quickly realized his hands and feet were anchored to the corners of the bed. He jerked at the straps violently.

He glared in Gwendolyn's direction. He was furious and frustrated as he demanded "What the fuck is going on?! Let me go!"

He continued to struggle. Henry's reaction violent reaction was predicted. The proper precautions were taken to ensure everyone's safety.

Gwendolyn rose to her feet and maintained a calm tone. "Henry, please calm yourself. I will undo the straps after we have had a small chat. Please relax, you are safe."

He stopped thrashing and took a deep breath. Gwendolyn continued. "Henry, do you remember your last day on earth?"

He glared at her wide eyed, unbelieving. "That's right, your last day on earth. You're now on an inter-dimensional ship called ROM. It's your home now. I realized this is confusing to you. Soon it will all makes sense."

Henry's gaze remained fixed on the beautiful speaker. "I guess I'll have to take your word for that" he said while making several smaller tugs at the binding straps. She took the hint and undid the buckles. He began massaging his wrists when they came free, his mind was reeling. He told himself to be calm, how bad could it be? He was alone with a gorgeous blonde sporting the body of a goddess.

"Can you stand for me Henry?"

Without speaking he sat and turned to stand. He was painfully aware of his nakedness. Instinctually his hands worked together to conceal his manhood.

Gwendolyn chuckled and turned towards the uniform hanging by the chair. She brought it to him and turned her head as he slipped effortlessly in to its perfect fit.

"Come with me Henry." She said with a smile.

He followed her through a door that suddenly appeared. His eyebrows arched in amazement as they passed through its threshold. They proceeded down a long dimly lit hallway. Another door manifested itself and guided them through to a kind of mess hall.

Gwendolyn scanned the rows of tables. They were dotted with randomly seated diners. Spotting her party, she signaled Henry with a gentle pat on the arm and gestured with her head for him to follow. She led him to a small group of people laughing and obviously enjoying their meals. Gwendolyn had called for a meeting at 12:30 and it appeared everyone was present and on time.

"Good afternoon, everyone." The seated attendees turned their attention to Gwendolyn. There were murmurs about the handsome man that accompanied her.

"Good afternoon!" they all chimed in unison.

Gwendolyn placed a hand on Henry's shoulder and smiled as she introduced him. "Everyone, I would like to introduce to you the newest addition to our ROM family. His name is Henry."

They greeted him enthusiastically. He smiled and nodded at them all. Gwendolyn invited Henry to take a seat, and then she joined him. He scanned his fellow table mates. They consisted of two young teenagers and a beautiful young woman. Gwendolyn's voice took on a serious tone as she spoke.

"Henry, I want you to know that Laqueesha, Tyrone and Allison here are all quite new two ROM as well. They are adjusting quickly." She smiled at her three favorite pupils.

Ally looked at Henry with sincerity and understanding as she spoke. "Henry, your first day is very confusing. Nothing seems real. But trust me when I say things will become clear soon. You will consider this all quite normal."

Henry had turned his attention to her while she spoke. "Thank you, Ally, I'm not there yet, but I'm looking forward to it." To his surprise, he found himself lost in her beautiful green eyes. She had the face of an angel, it was flawless, as if straight out of a fantasy. Everyone at the table noticed the instant attraction between them. Laqueesha nudged Tyrone with a gentle elbow. He nudged her back and they smiled widely. Gwendolyn blushed slightly as they all found themselves in an uncomfortable silence. Gwendolyn spoke abruptly, startling everyone back into the moment.

"Henry, you must be famished!" he turned his attention in her direction.

"Yes, more so than ever!"

Laqueesha was quite excited to fill him in on the nutritional aspects of living on ROM. She gushed with enthusiasm.

"Pick anything you want! Anything! All the food here has the same nutrition, so you can eat anything, and it won't be bad for you!"

Tyrone chimed in with excitement. "It don't matter if you have a salad with no dressing or an entire pound of bacon topped with extra grease, it's all made from the same stuff!"

Henry furrowed his brow and looked at Gwendolyn. She laughed and told him it was true and that she would explain it in more detail soon. Henry's hunger pains suggested the steak and eggs. He never enjoyed a meal more.

Gwendolyn escorted Henry down the dim hall to the conference room. She hesitated and turned to him before entering .

"Henry, this is where we bring new recruits from earth for an introductory tour. We introduce them to basic information about ROM. Things like environmental makeup, economic and social structure. But we're doing things a bit different with you today."

Henry's eyes widened, his attention on Gwendolyn's unusually stoic expression. She then passed through the door and signaled him with a wave for him to follow.

Henry spent his final years on earth fighting for the

restoration of the American dream. He fought alongside other patriots of the United States. The goal was to regain control from the hostile take over by China. The leaders of ROM recognized his dedication, leadership qualities and sheer bravery. They selected him to be recruited from the earth existing in the year 2045.

They entered the sparse room. James was waiting at a table that hosted three chairs. He rose from the one he had been occupying. Gwendolyn and Henry approached, and he extended a welcoming hand.

"Hello Henry, welcome. Please both of you take a seat." They complied.

"I'm going to cut to the chase Henry." James stated in an earnest tone. "We need to skip the usual gentle and gradual introduction to ROM that most recruits receive."

Gwendolyn shifted in her seat, as if bracing for Henry's pending reactions. Henry felt a twinge of nervous anticipation flood his body. Was he extremely curious? Or was he just plain scared?

"Time is of the essence, not here on ROM, but on earth. On ROM we don't exist on a timeline. Earth on the other hand does."

Henry felt as if his entire faced had formed into a large question mark. He looked from James to Gwendolyn and back again.

"May I ask what the hell you're talking about?!" Henry blurted with a strong tone of annoyance.

James slapped the open palms of his hands firmly on the tabletop, startling its occupants.

"Henry, we need your cooperation immediately! We went

to the earth existing in the year 2045 to recruit you. You are the key to the success of our mission!" Henry grew more impatient.

"What the fuck are you talking about?! You say you're gonna cut to the chase, so cut to the fucking chase!"

Gwendolyn interjected. "Henry, please let us explain" she paused and stroked his hand. "We need your help. We want you to lead our handpicked human army. You will return to earth before the year 2085, The date of its scheduled extinction."

"Now that, is cutting to the chase!" He ran his spread fingers from his forehead to the back of his head leaving tracks through his hair.

19

Ski Bunny Wipeout

Then peace will guide our planet, and love will rule the stars. ~
The 5th Dimension

.

Theodor Kaluza added another spatial dimension to account for the electromagnetic force. Very simply by adding another column and row to Einstein's metric tensor for General Relativity. That gives us a 5 x 5 metric tensor that includes an additional spatial dimension that the electricity may be inside of. It was quite nicely done. It suited everyone just fine, even Einstein. It's called the Electro-Magnetic Vector Potential.

It's not the end of the journey to higher dimensions. They thought they were complete. Time for the arts and retirement. By adding the 5th dimension for electro-magnetism. Both Einstein's Field Equations and Maxwell's equations fit together perfectly when you have them all together.

Now we know everything!

Unfortunately, rain falls according to gravity, but the drops are probabilistic where they will land. We don't live in a static universe. Our life is probabilistic. Let's blame it all on David Hilbert. The problem with the 5th dimension is the Einstein Hilbert action for quantum gravity. I left out the equation because I didn't even understand it. So actually, we are not done. There's no time for arts and entertainment yet.

We have to account for Sir Isaac Newton's pesky gravity. We have a place for gravity, but not with our massive and tiny things. Einstein, Maxwell, and Kaluza, with a bit of monkey wrench from Kline, account for our big glorious Universe. Except we found some little stuff. They are called particles, which are parts of atoms.

***

"The snow is a perfect powder today. Most days are slush,

followed by afternoon ice." Danny thought as he took the last drag.

The joint fluttered down to the snow. Watching the roach fall was pleasant. He almost forgot to lift up his tips and prepare to exit the chair lift. That would leave the wrong impression on Cindy. Who was one chair behind him.

Cindy was the cutest girl on the ski bus. He realized he didn't have much chance to score the coveted seat next to her on the way home. Giving up without a fight was not a trait Danny was known for.

"I'll do my best to sit with her. Some other dude might get the chair, but nobody will try harder."

Danny put the brakes on with a snowplow then twirled to a stop. Turning to watch Cindy exit the lift. She was slender. Even with a down jacket and bibs, she appeared lovely and delicate. The pink jacket, black pants of the bibs and boots didn't make her look any larger.

"Dainty, dolled out, delightful, delicious." Danny worked through the letters thinking of words to describe his crush.

Deceptive and devilish never came to mind as he continued to work his way through the Ds.

"Diamonds! In the future, this girl will be worth her weight in them, but today she is a snow bunny."

Danny was caught by surprise. He had been daydreaming and staring. Cindy was off the lift. She skied down the ramp like a pro. When she came to a stop in front of Danny, she fell. It was a gloriously clumsy wipe-out. She fell to the left. The fresh morning powder accepted her willingly. The only visible sign of her existence were the skis. Still attached to boots, they crossed like helicopter blades. The blades jutting out of the snow. Cindy was submerged in the powder. In a remote area, this could be a life-threatening situation. At the ski area, in front of Danny, it became a wonderful opportunity.

Danny reached into the dry powder snow. His hands followed the contours of Cindy's leg. Her hips were a wondrous goal, but he did not dwell there. Lingering to catch a feel of her perfectly shaped teenage buns was not the right thing to do. His fingers did glide over the target. Mentally aware and cataloging the experience for future reference. Danny's hands continued to her shoulders. Cindy could not have weighed more than ninety pounds. It was a cinch to scoop up her form with both of his hands around her. He put his hands under her arms, and gracefully pulled her body erect.

The snow had muffled the sound. Cindy was screaming, terrified from the experience. Danny was still holding her. Both of his hands tightly grasping her breasts.

"Let go of my boobs!" Cindy screamed.

Danny immediately complied. If his face hadn't already been red from the wind and the morning cold. It would have turned red from the embarrassment. He hadn't been aware of his hands on her breasts because of the fluffy down jacket. Everyone at the top of the lift was now informed that he had copped a feel. It wasn't fair. Sure he had felt her buns during the rescue. He did not linger. His heart had been in the right place. Now he'd be considered a deviant. Danny would be damned to an eternity of stares and comments behind his back. The result of doing the right thing. His neighbors would be told that he was a sexual predator. He would have to register every time he moved, and he hadn't even attended college yet.

"Damn it! I am a virgin. I can't be in this much shit already in life." Danny heard the words coming out of his lips as he said them. There was no filter in his mind. If he had been entirely sober, those words would not have left his mouth. The marijuana was kicking in, and he had spoken exactly what he was thinking audibly. The world heard he was a virgin. The realization that he was experiencing grass paranoia finally became clear to the teen boy. It was not his first time smoking a joint. He felt relief at that thought and looked at Cindy. Her hair was mussed. Her hat was missing. She had a wild look in her eyes. The terror had been real, and now she was safe.

"My hero! I thought I was going to die." Cindy said, turning in the arms of her rescuer.

She promptly pulled his head down and placed a wet kiss on the tip of Danny's nose. After which, she boldly stated. "Skunk! I smell skunk. Did you smoke weed? Give me some."

This gave Danny's ego a needed boost. At least he still had a joint rolled and tucked into his jacket's waterproof sleeve pocket. He would prove to himself that he has what it takes to get a girlfriend. It may be super cold, but Cindy was the hottest chick on the slopes, and Danny was on track. The fast track to take her home tonight.

"Not here Cindy, the Ski Patrol is strict. If they catch you smoking dope, you're off the slope. Your parents will be informed, and you won't be on the ski bus the rest of the season."

"Oh my G! Danny! You are totally paranoid." Quipped Cindy, tossing her blond hair back. "Did you see my hat anywhere?"

"It's gone with the wind Cindy. Use mine. I don't need it.

Let's ski down the trail. We'll find a safe place to fire up a doo-bie."

Danny took his black wool ski cap and placed it on her head. Pulling the warm wool down over her already bright red ears.

"Let's go Cindy, I'll follow you."

Cindy made it to the West Trail without falling again. Danny was in heaven. He was so proud to have made it this far.

20

The Ski Trail

The past is not solid. It is probabilistic in the same way as the future. The history can be rewritten. Zero is an arbitrary edge of reality. The absolute absence of speed, and distance area focused on zero is the absolute lack of energy. This is a collapsed wave. The measured point that has no measure. Some might call it the empty set, but the empty set filled with zero is not empty. It is as the vacuum may be construed to be empty. The emptiness of outer space's void is full of the majority of the universe's weight. Zero is the circle and the point of which time emerges. The place where time and space come together. With the infinite contraction of non-being and the infinite expansion of being. The meeting point is full of energy. Energy similar to the dark energy of space. The energy convergence of time and space that our basis and dance of life prances about.

Atlas would be released from a substantial portion of his burden. Approaching 96% of his back-breaking burden would be gone. Zero would be a big favor for him. Instead of being a barrier, zero is the fulcrum of the balance between the yin and the yang of reality. The arrow of time doesn't exist in reality. It is only a representation of observed reality. The thundering clap of time banging on zero would otherwise wake up 96% of the reality that is stored energy at zero. Instead, like any other particle in our probabilistic universe, the tachyon passes by zero into the past. The intersections of the hyper polygonal volumes of reality gracefully accept the input into the intersections of multiple Minkowski spacetime bubbles. Happily free from observation half of the time, the tachyons vibrate their dance in the forever space of reality.

It is about time. About time for what? Any time is anytime, and that's for certain. Once the ability to traverse time becomes apparent, it didn't take much time for time to become obsolete. Those characters locked and lost in the past soon broke free from the bindings placed on them by the physicists and engineers that formulated time one way. Elegant math was used conveniently assigning conventions to the minus sign forcing its disappearance from reality. The 4d matrix of our visible universe doesn't work with the practicality of dimensions beyond 4. Time travel requirements are above the 4th dimension. The Lorentz invariance breaks down and allows for the fluid movement of acceleration and retardation of time and its associated particles. None of this matters if you are in the process of being rescued from the side of a mountain. Which is a situation that makes believing in the flatness of the universe unlikely.

***

Cindy paused at the entrance to the forest. The trailhead was marked with a warning sign in front of her. "Warning! Ski Patrol does not monitor or patrol this trail! Enter at your own risk."

"Here goes nothing." Said Cindy as she leaned back, sitting into the boots which fit high up her calves.

With her tips up, she started down the trail. The trees and beautiful powder snow muffled the sounds of the excited crowd on the main run. Soon she could only hear her breath and Danny's skis crunching louder than hers to the rear. His body approaching 200 pounds compressed the snow under his skis. Cindy thought the sound was like chomping down on a bowl of Captain Crunch. She was already getting the munchies without taking one drag off of Danny's joint.

Her mother didn't make breakfast anymore. Her jobs took up to much of her time. Even going to the market had become difficult. Time is a commodity. Wasting time, taking moments to relax and enjoy life were little luxuries ordinary moms don't have time for.

Communication with Mom had become a note exchange.

"I love you, Cindy."

"I love you, Mom."

Reapply, rinse, repeat, like the daily shampoo and conditioner. Conversations with Mom had become infrequent. When they happened to see each other face to face, the conversation was minimalistic. Hugs, kisses on the cheeks, and a quick "I love you." As one or the other stepped out the apartment door.

Conversation wasn't more than the slips of paper they traded back and forth. For what reason did more trees need to die? To buy more notebooks that gathered the same repetitive message day in and day out. Surely one, or both of them could recycle a previous message. Using the same paper, again and again, would convey the same thought. I love you, Mom. She didn't have to repeat it over and over. It was a waste of resources and time. Except she had to. Cindy loved her mother dearly and understood her sacrifices to keep her in school.

When Dad had died, it had changed both of them. They had all ate breakfast that morning. It had been a hot day. August was when summer truly came in, and the mercury was already ¾ of the way up the thermometer. Mom smiled and giggled happily at Dad's jokes.

Cindy remembered the breakfast vividly. There was the smell of the bacon and the hot syrup Mom made on the stovetop. Her perspiring forehead dripping sweat droplets into the syrup, which erupted each time with a sparkle and hiss. The apron and the pretty panties covered with hearts and sexy lips let her firm butt jiggle its little dance, opposite of the spatula shuffle which scrambled eggs in the pan. Cindy had been mesmerized. She wondered if she could ever be as beautiful as her. Both Daddy and her stared. Of course, for different reasons. It was likely her father was getting horny watching Mommy's morning breakfast "show." Cindy thought she couldn't wait to be just like Mom.

That's when the glass of the kitchen window had broke. Gunfire in the street erupting as Daddy jerked, slumping forward. His head hit the coffee spilling it all over the table. Mommy's pretty panties turned utterly wet. Red with her father's blood. He had died that day, Smiling and looking at his beautiful wife.

Cindy would kill trees. She would waste ink and the valuable resource of time every day forever. Writing "I love you, Mom" on a piece of paper. She didn't care if the entire world turned into a desert, and they could only drink ink. She would waste the last scrap of paper. Using the last drop of ink to write. "I love you, Mom." one last time.

Thump! Cindy heard the trees thump and felt the spray of powder snow on her cheeks. The tree lay directly in her path. It was a rather large Douglas fir. Cindy shrieked in fright, leaning back farther on her skis. Cindy's skis and legs fluttered like a cartoon figure slipping on a banana peel.

Danny saw it all. Cindy's comedy pratfall ended suddenly with another scream. This one, unlike the previous one, was shockingly loud. The Douglas fir was covered with bushy bows of green. Except for a few frozen dead branches bare of needles jutting out like brown spears.

The pain was unbearable. Cindy found herself butted up to the tree. Her head down the hill again with her legs, boots, and skis up in the air like a helicopter for the second time today. Ordinarily, this would be hilarious. Except for this time, she lay on her back. Looking at the predicament her melancholy daydreaming had gotten her into. She screamed again, then stopped because screaming caused even more pain.

What she saw and felt would put her into shock shortly in her current state of coherence, as short-lived as it would be. She muttered one joke.

"At least I won't die a virgin."

Danny heard it as he pushed through the powder towards her. He took off his skis Next to Cindy. Surveying the situation, Danny could see this was a life or death emergency. The Douglas fir's spearlike branch jutted out of Cindy's down jacket. It penetrated her crotch and pushed through all the way to her stomach. Where its jagged broken end poked at least twelve inches out of her stomach. Cindy had crazy eyes. She stared at the branch, then at Danny, then back again to the branch which was not going to let her go.

"Help me, Danny! I don't want to die."

Danny didn't know what to do, so he improvised. Taking her skis off one by one, then punched them into the snow. This was helpful immediately. It relieved some of the heavy pressure on her legs. Then he took the poles off of her gloved hands. The straps had stayed on, and the poles crossed above her head. It would have been a seductive pose if this had been another time and place. Cindy's legs spread, and arms raised above her head.

Danny quickly stopped thinking like that. He was ashamed to have even thought that in this horrible situation.

She brought her hands up. Reaching between her legs, and felt the branch that penetrated her body like a bad anime tentacle. She looked to her stomach, pulling at her gloves. Cindy was trying to remove them to feel the damage to her body.

Danny said, "No, Cindy. You have to stay warm. Keep your gloves on. Don't worry. It will be okay. I'll go get help. Wait for me. I'll be right back."

Cindy stopped talking. Her terrified tearful eyes stared at him. Danny had never seen someone in such a pitiful position. Picking up his cap, he bent down, brushed her hair to the side with his mitten, and gave her a soft kiss on the forehead. Then he pulled the hat onto her head again.

"I'll be back with the ski patrol Cindy. You'll be okay. "

He fastened his skis, thump-thump and skied away like a crazy man. He had to get help. This was rapidly turning into the worst day ever, and the day had just started.

2 1

Rattlesnake

We have a paradox. The Einstein, Podolski Rosen paradox. Do we even need to know if this is certain? Indeed, everyone wants to believe, But really, what for? All these big, bad, and beautiful black holes are so far away from us.

Well, we can test parts of the results of entanglement. So maybe we can't test the entanglement of black holes light-years away from us. We can test entangled particles. Numerous experiments have been done to prove precisely that. The tiniest of particles show connectedness if many tiny particles can be entangled. How about the black hole? Einstein and Rosen thought so, and with the help of Podolski, we have the interesting acronym EPR.

What is "Base-rate neglect?" It sounds so deplorable. Nobody wants to be neglected. That is not really what it means. Ignoring the probability that something is true is common. People do not like to believe the numbers. They would prefer to hear exciting words, shocking things. Then look at the numbers calmly and make a decision based on fact.

Keep an open mind and don't succumb to thoughts that are not statistically provable. Our experiment is grand and encompasses our lives. We can not function effectively without a moral compass. However, don't allow your predisposition and prior training to interfere with the value of a good experiment. Don't let your judgment interfere with the results. Your personal bias may contaminate them, but your personal bias might show the right path to take.

The pursuit of math must be made in measured doses. Otherwise, your ability to function in decent company might suffer. It should only be indulged in or on a marked time schedule and with a memorable attitude. Remembering whichever axiom or theorem you study is more important than spending so much time and becoming tired, forgetting the subject's substance.

It's easier to learn by breaking up subjects into subgroups. This is one of the secret keys to studying. Break it up, spend some time with one pen, then don't forget to stand up, walk to the shelf. Inking up something else is prudent behavior. You may find some antique pen on that shelf that deserves your attention. The ghost of some forgotten soul could come to your hand when you hold that ancient relic. Words may stream out the nib that never would have if you hadn't changed your writing instrument. Follow the pen and see where it takes you.

The pen is mightier than the sword. When the pen can't write, it is seriously a dangerous situation for society. By removing the ability for individuals to be heard, humanity is left in a precarious position.

People need a place to express themselves freely. It seems there are few places are left on earth for the expression of individual dissent. America is left. Perhaps a few more places, but time will tell as to how many survive. We may enter another dark age for mankind if we aren't careful with the path we walk towards censorship.

In the past, there have been trials by the press and Congress. Not that long ago, Hollywood had a "blacklist" based on political viewpoints that were not popular. It did not require a conviction in court to be on that list. It was a shameful time in American history, that is a time which seems to be repeating now.

Stand tall, remember what your parents taught you about

good and evil, about right and wrong. Do the right thing and damn the haters. You can't help them. They are on the dark side. Haters are going to hate. I am not talking about acute hate. I am talking about that toxic, chronic hater. The one that dooms and hates all day long. They are the enemy. They are the enemy that will lead you down the path to losing your soul.

America is left; Americans are indivisible. We are an immutable force that can't be broken apart. When we are separated or segregated, the weight of our mass brings us back together. We stand together in times of National trouble like a single unbreakable force of will. Except when we are tricked. We tend to be trusting and naive to the world. Our European brothers are tetchy, touched with that cynical despair of thousands of years of trickery by their nobility.

America lets her freedom ring loudly and clearly so as not to stifle the independence of our great nation. Liberty being her fundamental right from the very beginning. The citizenry takes ownership of their rights and shares their national experience. It is our right and not a privilege to put words on paper and share those words with others. They don't have to be well thought out. They can be a train wreck of ideas, yet we can share them because it is our fundamental first right that our constitutional backbone is built upon.

Other parts of the world do not enjoy this right. Many Americans take it for granted and don't realize the danger of stepping on this part of our legal heritage in order to win a small victory at the moment; thinking about what happens tomorrow and living just for today's simple, shallow victory is the only thing on their minds.

Americans give the silenced members of humanity a place where they may write their political speech without fear. Without a penalty for having controversial views. Expression of controversial viewpoints is the most protected right Americans have. When that is taken from them, what happens to the world? Our precious freedom depends on this. Our sacred rights count on it. Our battle flags embrace the theme. The memes of history were not digital. They were analog and flew fluttering in the breeze above battlefields where our grandfathers fought, bled, and died.

Those battle flags with words such as "Don't tread on me" are digitally recreated these days with words like "Don't step on snek." Cute words, but important advice. The American is a rattlesnake. Our ancestors knew it. The snake that keeps to himself, unless provoked. When provoked, a biting poisonous wound is the result.

The temptation to silence, or suppress the opinion of the ordinary man, if it goes against the narrative that may effect your own views, must be incredibly enticing for a rich man. However, controlling the library of humanity should have a certain amount of obligation. That obligatory behavior being absent could cause irreparable damage to society. Generations could pass before freedom pokes its head out of whatever dark barrel it was stored in. The chaos of liberty will eventually find its way into the light, but to those that lost it. It will be gone forever. It won't return to those that don't deserve to have it. Some future that exists where freedom and liberty will shine through again. Those that give it up won't see it happen again. Their lifetime of security will result in the loss of Liberty, and that is not worth it. Security is not a right. It is not fundamentally guaranteed. Only our pursuit of happiness is guaranteed, certified as a right by our founding fathers. Who considered it God-given, as do many Americans still. Let's hope that America remains free. The alternative is a world of slavery for generations to come.

22

God Hears Danny's Prayer

Danny skied like a wild man. Straight down the trail, moguls be damned, his knees bent sitting back in his boots and poles hitting all at the right time. This was the best ski run he had ever made. What a terrible time to be into it. He had to get help fast for Cindy. He skied on, hoping to spot a red ski patrol jacket, someone with a radio to make a call. There wasn't any cellphone signal off of the main runs. The slopes had limited signal, but the side trails had nothing.

This was the first time Danny had been down this trail. Cindy seemed to have known where she was going. He just followed along like a stupid dog healing, following the pheromone leash that Cindy wafted at him. He was smitten and hooked on her. Nothing was going to stop that. Now he had to save her. He would be her hero forever.

Knees hitting his chest and poles planting and turning, his hips and shoulders pointed down the slope to find a rescue. There was hypnotic zen to the rhythm of it all. The trail was perfect. The snow was just right. This would have been the most fantastic day of his life at another time. Skiing down this quiet, beautiful trail, he hadn't given it a thought as to why this slope was deserted on such a busy ski day. It was actually dangerous. This was a deadly run. There had been more warning signs, but they were buried under the snow, and no one had bothered to upright and retrieve them. Who would be so stupid as to take an unmarked trail on the side of a mountain in the wilderness to smoke some dope and flirt with a girl? Danny was just that stupid, and this was a trail to nowhere. It didn't lead back to the main run, the lift, or even a rope tow. There wasn't a lodge at the bottom of the trail. It led into a depression. It may as well have been the pit of hell, and Danny started to slow down. The grade of the hill reduced, and he was at the end of the run.

It was then that Danny realized just how fucked he was. To the front of him was a granite wall. Behind him, the snowy, wonderful, and steep trail he had just flawlessly hit like a giant slalom master. To the right, there was pure snow and ice. Looking up, he estimated it to be 2000 feet snow wall looking back at him. It was lovely fresh snow. How it stuck to the mountain was incredible gravity-defying beauty that only God could construct. He was at the bottom of a natural wonder. To the left was just impossible. Open sky and dizzying height made his stomach turn. He could base jump it easily, except he was fresh out of parachutes today. Even if he had a parachute, he wouldn't know how to do it. Base Jumping was something he had only seen on TV.

He remembered seeing the video of the guy jumping off of the New River Gorge Bridge in Wisconsin or Nebraska. He couldn't remember the state. Maybe it was Virginia. It didn't matter. He wasn't there. He was here, and here sucked right now.

Cindy would probably die, and he might too if he couldn't climb his way out of here. Here being nowhere. The end of the road. That last place on earth to be when you were in a hurry.

He knew the highway was at the bottom of the cliff. He knew the main slope was at the top of the wall of snow. He could choose between making a descent down a cliff in ski boots, which would likely be a fall to certain death, or climbing the fresh wall of snow. He might be able to do that in the skis. It was going to take some time. There wasn't a choice. He had to go up the snow wall if he wanted to rescue Cindy. If he wanted to live, he had to do it as well.

His ears were starting to burn. He remembered that he'd given his hat to Cindy.

"What a day, what a way to spend what should have been the best day. " He said to himself as he began the climb up the steep snowy slope.

His buzz from the joint he smoked that morning was gone entirely. The adrenaline had ruined that. Now serious, he spread his legs open like a duck, picking up his left ski and putting it a foot up the hill. His right ski planted another foot above that, and he got into the groove. This was going to be challenging, but it was doable. He wasn't going to give up on it. Left foot up, right foot up, plant the ski, and lean into the hill. He dropped the poles, they were of no use, and he used his hands to climb. Basically, Danny crawled up the mountain. His hips screamed, but he ignored that pain. It was nothing compared to a hard wrestling practice. He just climbed and climbed.

He wondered about the slope of the hill. Or would you call it a grade? It was confusing, and he never paid attention in class. He remembered bits and pieces of the formulae; The lessons and the ski bus science about it. There was a sweet spot for ski runs. The slopes ranging from 10% to 30% degrees descending anything over 30% was crazy difficult. When you approach 45%, you are at your highest risk of causing an avalanche. The snow stuck to the mountains easily but could break away. Even a loud noise might cause it to tumble to the bottom of the mountain. Danny realized that this was fresh snow, and he was ascending a slope between 30 and 45%. He stopped and said a prayer.

"God, oh God. I have screwed up so badly. I don't know what I can do, or how I can finish this. Please God, oh God. Help me figure this out and keep me strong enough to get to the top. Thank you God. Amen." He finished putting in plenty of God, and oh God, just like the pastor did at church. He crossed himself like the priests in the movies and continued up the steep slope.

His stomach felt the drop first. The snow had decided that the weight of Danny was just enough additional mass to generate an event, and he slid about 20 feet down the hill. The snow he was clutching fell with him. It was only a second, or so it seemed, but he felt it, like jumping off of the high dive at the pool. Then he stopped. It was just a minor snow slide. The bit of snow he clung to had decided to move down the hill. It included him in the journey. Nothing was harmed, and it was hard to tell that he had moved at all. Except for the falling feeling in his stomach. That awful sinking feeling that he craved in the summer. He felt it on the roller coaster and screamed, and of course, it was the fun part of jumping off of the diving board. Here it was terrifying. He was in the middle of it, clinging to the snow. Danny cried.

His father's voice rang in his red stinging ears. "You can't finish anything if you quit. Winners don't quit, son. Even if you want to stop, you have to keep it up."

Dad was always so sincere and sappy. He tried hard, but it always came off like something out of a John Wayne movie. Basically, he always just meant. Do your best, and be a good man because bad guys are losers. It isn't worth it to be a bad guy. He never smiled when he talked. He couldn't remember seeing Dad smile. He went to work in the morning. He came home at night. Sleep and repeat. He just kept going. Ever since Mom had died, he just lived like a robot. Robot dad wakes up at 4:30, drinks coffee, smokes a cigarette. Followed by a shit, shower, and a shave. Then out the door at 5. Saturday night was beer.

They both slept in every Sunday, then went to church. Danny always went with him. This was the time that they spent together. Walking down the road to church on Sunday to St. Paul's Lutheran Church was not that special, but it was special to Danny. Mom's funeral had been there. Dad and Danny walked, every Sunday since. It didn't matter if the sun was out or if it was raining. They walked every Sunday to church. Neither of them considered walking to the car and making the drive. It was only a mile, and they walked together silently on Sundays. It was the one thing they could do together and identify with. About the only change to the routine had been a few years ago when Dad had stopped holding his hand when they walked. Other than that, the walking was as much a part of the religious experience for Danny as the sermon.

"Focus, you idiot!" Danny said to himself.

The mountainside was no place to become melancholy, and Cindy was counting on him. He continued up the hill, determined to save her life. He didn't realize how close he was to losing his own.

23

Geronimo

Danny was oblivious to the tachyon buildup as it burst overheard. Like other humans, he could not sense their activity. He just lived in the ordinary reality that Aristotle and Newton left for the average guy on the street. Inevitably the snow would fall, and when it dropped, the weight was felt. That is the reality Danny lived in. He had made a bad choice. The alternative had been worse. Bad or worse were his only options. As pitiful as they were. Danny had chosen bad over worse. His desire to rescue Cindy had come to a sudden stop. With a thud, bad had turned into worst. There would be no more climbing. He was stuck, and it sucked. His left leg dangled a clean snap of the femur in the light breeze. The snow had fallen for the second time. This time Danny was not so lucky. He sat partially covered in ice and snow. His leg was broken, and every part of his body was screaming in pain.

Cindy stood in soft but glowing light. Her dress was white and cascaded softly to the lush green grass below. Her silky blonde hair flowed over her delicate shoulders. She held a bouquet of beautiful pink and pale-yellow roses, studded with baby's breath. Long pink silk ribbons cascaded softly below the bouquet. Her angelic face was filled with love. Her china doll skin was flawless, and the sparkle in her blue eyes was breathtaking. The smile she wore was inviting, practically begging him to join her. His eyes never left hers as he grew closer to her beauty. They reached out for each other's hands and grasped them warmly. He drew her in close, and they locked eyes. Suddenly Cindy let go of her grip on his hands and rose hers to his cheeks. She held them in her soft grasp and spoke directly into his soul.

"Danny, my love, it just wasn't meant to be." The dream then burst like a bubble.

All of this trouble was over the illegal use of marijuana. Danny was a bad boy. If he'd been good, then he would not be smoking the ganja. Cindy would never have been tempted to smoke out with him. She would not be dying and crying, laying in the snow a couple of thousand feet above him. She would be riding the chairlift, giggling, and skiing down the main run like all the other kids.

That being said, it was all done. Danny couldn't change the past any more than anyone else could change what had already happened. The pain was crazy bad; if any time was the right time, now was the perfect time to fire up a doobie. No excuse was necessary. Obviously, he was going to die, and Cindy would die too because he had been so stupid. Nothing more was left except to get stoned and slowly freeze. Danny pulled off his gloves, resting them on the snow beside him, and reached into his sleeve pocket for his last rolled joint. It was still there and miraculously undamaged. Which is more than could be said for Danny's lanky teenage body.

The broken leg was the apparent damage. Flicking the lighter was effort and pain. It took a while, but he could finally get the joint lit. He held it between his lips with his teeth as added protection against loss. He did not want to drop the roach. It was his last and would be his last forever. Of this, he was sure. He could barely breathe in the rich marijuana smoke. The skunk flavor forced a cough when he finally got a lungful. The cough brought separate pain. He must have a broken rib. He thought nonchalantly while sucking in more smoke. The pain didn't disappear with the high that was coming on, but it felt distant. He didn't care that his body was all torn up. Here he was on the edge of the world, looking out into the Cascades. People would pay for this view. From his vantage point, he could see nearly to forever. It was a little dizzying. That may have been the effect of the THC taking hold. He coughed a bit more, still feeling the pain in his leg and the lungs. His mind was distracted, and despite the pain, he thought of other things. He thought about Cindy and what could have happened between them. How it would have been great and grand. His dad would have smiled when he brought her home, a steady girlfriend to make the stink of a male-only household just a little sweeter. He didn't actually know much about Cindy, but she seemed just perfect. Well, she was just perfect until she wiped out into the tree. By now, she must be dead. He hadn't been the knight coming to rescue her. He had just been the boy that ruined her and brought her short life to a tragic frozen end. Tears started to stream down his cheeks. He wasn't getting happy with his last high on earth. He was becoming sorrowful and full of sadness. What a perfectly awful way to spend the day, broken hanging off the side of a mountain, freezing to death, stoned and despondent.

Danny felt it in his stomach first as the snow shelf finally gave up its fight against the gravity of the situation. He was falling and high at the same time.

He croaked out a "Geronimo!" as loudly as he could. He wasn't going to die screaming like a sissy.

Then all of a sudden, he wasn't falling. He was soaring like a bird. He looked down on the ski resort, and then he was inside. Inside where? He didn't know. His warmups disintegrated along with his long johns and sweatshirt. He was naked, broken, confused, and floating in a dark room that wasn't quite dark.

He heard, "prepare of emergency purification." Coming from a metallic voice.

Then blackness overtook him as the shock of the situation fully set in. Danny passed out unconscious. Before any gas was necessary. The technician took note of his condition. Pressing the emergency red button would summon advanced medical support who would arrive at the medical pod almost immediately from whatever time situation they were experiencing. Danny's young body would be nursed back to health, and he would be capable of running, jumping, and even skiing again if he thought taking the risk was worth it after this disaster of an escapade.

Healing Danny's head would prove much harder. He wasn't a quitter. Losing his Cindy was formidable grief. His head could not deal with the loss of this young woman. Her frozen carcass was gnawed down to the bones by hungry forest creatures and left to a small blurb in the history, which Danny found shortly after being introduced to ROM's equivalent to the Internet.

24

French Dip and Fries

I've never liked driving. In fact, I hate it. The bus goes everywhere I need to go. I don't have a car payment, pay for insurance, never stop for gas, and never have to hunt for a parking space. So, when Chuck came up with the idea of a road trip, I was less than interested.

"Would you bring me the chips?" Chuck billowed from the Plaid green monster he hadn't moved from in over 2 hours.

" Sure," I chimed sarcastically, then added, anything else, your majesty?"

I rolled my eyes when he answered loudly, "And a Diet Coke."

I dropped ungracefully down on the worn recliner and tossed the sour cream and onion chip bag through the air. He caught it with a loud crinkly thud. Startled, Boyd scratched Chuck's pronounced belly on his frantic exit from the room.

"God damn it, Boyd!" he scolded while pulling the bag open.

I laughed and handed him the warm Diet Coke. He popped the top and took a big swig.

" He needs his claws clipped!" he stated through a guttural burp.

I was scrolling through the lineup of movies playing on cable when Chuck scared the shit out of me. He suddenly screamed with excitement. "Sleepless in Seattle!"

Sleepless in Seattle was his all-time favorite movie. The minute my heart started beating again, I quizzed him. "How many fucking times have you seen that stupid movie?"

He looked at me with an almost threatening stare. "As of this moment, or after tonight?"

At that, I knew what we were watching that evening. I

spent most of the movie scrolling through my phone. I would occasionally look up at Chuck. He was happy, stretched out with potato chip crumbs on his chest and a Turkey-shaped cat on his belly.

"Don't crumple that bag up," I said, quite amused. Prompting him to look at Boyd, then back at Meg Ryan.

The evening was extremely long and tedious for me, but not for Chuck. He was delighted as he savored the movie's ending. He sat blowing his nose and sobbing through tears of joy. I reached for the remote.

"No!" he squealed franticly.

"It's over, Chuck!"

"It's not completely over until the credits are done!" He whined while pulling out another clump of fresh tissues.

When the credits were over, he began to clap. Once again, my eyes rolled. At that, I decided to turn in and tossed him the remote.

"No, wait, I have an idea!" He squealed excitedly.

I could almost see the light from the bulb that went on in this head.

"Let's take a road trip to Seattle!"

"No," I said firmly and started towards my bedroom.

"Wait! Why not? It would be a blast!" He cooed.

"Well, let's see. Oh yeah, I don't have a car. Not only that, I hate driving. You can't drive, so I'm thinking you just had a really stupid fucking idea. Not to mention I can't leave Boyd alone."

Next thing you know, I'm in a rented Toyota Camry with an oversized fag and an equally rotund Siamese cat, cruising west on Interstate 90. We were only 20 minutes into our road trip when Boyd decided to use the litter box behind the driver seat on the floor. It set the tone for our entire journey.

If you make good time, without a lot of screwing around, the typical drive to Seattle should take about 8 to 9 hours. I knew in advance that we would not make good time. I was correct. It took us about 12 hours, plus the time we would sleep. That's right, 12 long hours of rancid farts, potty stops, and meal breaks.

Our first stop was a little over an hour into the drive. Chuck had googled touristy stops between Missoula and Seattle. Apparently, Saint Regis has a travel center. It features a gift shop, specialty ice cream, a live trout aquarium, and get this, free popcorn! Oh yes, we had to stop there. So, we did. Chuck got an ice cream cone despite the freezing November day. We both used the restroom and took the complimentary popcorn to go.

We settled back into the car. Chuck struggled to strap his seat belt because Boyd smelled the strawberry cheesecake ice cream on his breath and was trying his best to lick chuck's lips. Annoyed, Chuck hoisted the fat feline up onto the back of the seat, then gave him a gentle but firm shove into the back. This made for a miserable cat. Whenever Boyd becomes annoyed or angry, he expresses it by passing gas. Today was no exception. We decided to stop in Spokane to eat.

The ride to Spokane went pretty smooth. Chuck and Boyd snoozed on and off most of the way. I was glad they were unconscious when we reached the entrance to both passes. It was snowing, and being a nervous driver anyway, the last thing I needed was for Chuck To be freaking out in the seat beside me.

As I drove through Spokane, I considered waking Chuck. I was going to ask him what he wanted to eat. But I reconsidered. He was obviously in a deep sleep. After all, isn't it good advice to let sleeping dogs lie? Or maybe don't poke a bear with a stick? Anyway, I decided to keep quiet and continue to Ritzville. It was only about an hour up the road.

I pulled into Jake's cafe parking lot and was happy to see a parking space near the entrance. I shut off the engine and pulled out the key. My companions remained asleep.

"Chuck," I said in a loud voice while delivering a firm poke to his arm. Nothing. I tried a little bit louder. "Chuck!" and delivered a firmer poke.

His eyes flew open, and he turned to me, a startled look on his face. "Are we in Spokane?"

I shook my head no and told him we were in Ritzville. He instantly displayed his annoyance. This puzzled me slightly, and I asked him. "What? Do you have something against Ritzville?"

"You said we were gonna eat in Spokane; I wanted to go to Denny's!" He whined.

I told him he needed his rest, which put us one hour closer to Seattle. He seemed appeased. I turned to check the back seat. Boyd's big, blue, crossed eyes were open, and he yawned so big, it looked like his head was going to turn inside out. Without asking him, Chuck reached into the glove box. He retrieved a can of tuna-flavored Fancy Feast, pulled open the can, plopping its contents into Boyd's Tony the Tiger cereal bowl.

We opened the door to the restaurant and were greeted by warm air and the pleasant smell of fried hamburgers and apple pie. A young girl with a long brown ponytail and acne scars showed us to our seats. I had requested a table by the window to keep an eye on the car. I didn't want anybody messing with Boyd.

Chuck studied the menu, flipping it over and back several times as if it were going to be different with each turn. I knew what I wanted to order before I entered the establishment. I was hungry and was becoming impatient.

"Just fucking pick something, Chuck." I said in a firm whisper.

"OK, OK." He said with a slight sigh.

Nina, our waitress, placed a glass of water in front of each of us. She stood poised and ready with her little green-lined order book.

"Are you ready to order?" She said with a smile and a friendly tone.

Chuck snuck another quick glance at both sides of the menu and handed it to Nina.

"I'll have the chicken fried steak, but you can leave the seasonal vegetables off the plate. I would also like extra gravy and a side of fries." Nina had an amused look on her face as she jotted down his order.

She turned her attention to me.

"I'd like the French dip with fries," and with that, I handed her my menu.

With our orders placed, Chuck immediately plucked his phone from his pocket. After all, he had been asleep for two hours and needed to catch up on his social media platforms.

Nina brought our selections and set them in front of us. We switched our plates and began to eat. Chuck made noises of delight as he ate. I guess he liked it. Mine was also good, but I try to keep my food experiences to myself.

We finished our meals in what could be considered record time. Chuck sat back and burped loudly. I cringed when I noticed the elderly couple across from us look over in disgust. You should have seen their faces when he announced he had to take a shit before we left.

The car was pretty damn cold when we got back in. I started the engine and cranked the heat. It would be 2 1/2 hours to Snoqualmie Pass. If everything went smoothly, it took us 4. We pulled out of the snowy parking lot and headed west. I had made reservations to stay the night at the Snoqualmie Summit Inn. This leg of the journey would be a little more eventful. Boyd pooped again; Chuck farted more times than either of us cared to count. I drove, gagged, and asked myself repeatedly why the fuck I agreed to do this.

When we arrived at the inn, Chuck agreed that the least he could do was make the snowy trek into the office. He gave me a slightly resentful look and got out of the car. A cold whoosh of mountain air swept in and made Boyd's fur ripple. I waited semi patiently for his return. Boyd seemed to sense my anticipation. He climbed over the seat and plopped into the butt-warmed surface Chuck had abandoned. Then decided my lap was a better choice. I was happy to accept his warm girth. Finally, Chuck emerged from the building and hurried as fast as his plumpness allowed towards the car. Another whoosh of cold air followed him in as he slipped back into his seat.

"Room 104, around the back." He informed me, with a shiver in his voice.

We drove around the back and parked in our allotted space. Once the three of us were settled in the cozy room, we turned on the small plasma television set. The room was a bit dated but clean. It was kind of like being at home.

I felt my eyelids getting heavy. Boyd had made the end of chuck's bed his domain for the duration of our stay. I started to fall asleep. Chuck noticed and wasn't having it.

"Oh no, no, it's only 7:30!"

"Says the asshole who slept most of the way here!" I countered.

He waved a dismissive hand in my direction. He got up and gleefully grabbed the duffel bag he had packed that morning. After hoisting it onto his lap, he unzipped it, revealing its bulging contents. Smiling widely, he pulled a fifth of Skyy vodka from its depths. He held the bottle high over his head and proclaimed, "We're on vacation!"

I had to laugh. What the hell. He was right. We were on vacation. Half the bottle was gone in a flash. We were having a good time. We started getting a little bit restless, having had drunk ourselves past being tired. Another lightbulb went on in Chuck's head, and we found ourselves on a staggering walk through the snow. My drunken mind instantly took me back to the fateful New Year's Eve we spent together so many years ago. I didn't bring it up to him. I didn't want to bum him out, we were having fun, and I didn't want to spoil the mood. He can switch from extremely happy to crying very quickly. I was more than a little surprised when he suddenly did a little skip and blurted out, "The only way I could be happier right now is if I still had a dick!"

We both broke out in hysterical laughter. When I finally

caught my breath and took a little control of my composure, I suggested to him that we should go back to the room. We walked intentionally slow. It was nice. We talked and laughed. He noticed a snowbank that looked like a good place to lean back and rest against, so we did. Chuck leaned his head back on the soft, fresh snow. I watched his expression. It was full of what I can only describe as contentment. I smiled at his happiness.

I was suddenly startled. His expression changed dramatically from bliss to bewildered. His eyes were wide. He leaned forward in full attention mode. My gaze followed his into the clearing sky. The recent snowfall had given way to darkness speckled with bright, mesmerizing stars. The stars weren't what Chuck was focused on. Then I saw it. I don't know exactly what we were looking at, but I couldn't look away.

"Oh my God, what the hell is that?" He said with a slight gasp in a sober and soft tone.

I had no words to answer him. We sat and watched silently. For lack of a better description, they were some sort of orbs that illuminated a strange light. They started high in the sky and moved downwards toward the mountain's summit. Soon they disappeared behind the towering Douglas firs. I'm not sure when we returned to our room or how. We woke up early and continued our journey to Seattle.

The illusion persisted. Chuck couldn't forget its high-resolution space opera glowing moment. The pod crossed dimensionally with time and space moving about it like fluid. The pod remained in place, never moving from the deck of ROM. The observed only appeared to move to the observer.

25

Goodnight Mr. Hoffa

Ally woke slowly on what she perceived as an operating table. Naked, groggy, and beyond confused. She struggled to lift her body onto her elbows. Her vision was blurred. She blinked until her eyes cleared and could once again focus. She then scanned the room slowly. It was empty all around her but was filled with a dim light that didn't seem to come from anywhere. She strained to see the perimeter of the area, but it didn't seem to have any physical walls. Only complete darkness where they would typically be. She eases herself back down and laid flat. Her eyes squeezed tightly shut.

She whispered to herself. "What's happening to me?"

Suddenly aware of a presence right beside her, she could feel its heat slightly on her exposed skin. She slowly rolled her body in its direction, eyes still squeezed tight. Ally felt stiff and reluctant. Suddenly her lids began to part. As they slowly lifted, a woman was revealed, an extremely beautiful woman. Statuesque, wearing a long sleek silver jumpsuit, poured over what was a perfect form. Long blond silky curls spilled gracefully over her shoulders as she leaned in to get closer. The young newcomer was confused, her wide-eyed gaze locked on the tall beauty that began to speak softly.

"Hello, Allison. My name is Gwendolyn. I'm here to welcome you. I have been appointed as your transition officer." Ally started to reply but was hushed by one of Gwendolyn's long graceful fingers that pressed itself gently to her lips. Her soft words continued.

Don't worry. I know you are confused and full of questions. Please be patient; they will all be answered in due time."

"OK," Ally whispered. She felt safe with Gwendolyn.

Gwendolyn straightened to her full height and offered an outstretched hand to Ally. She asked,

" It's time to stand Allison, can you do that for me?"

Ally accepted the hand for assistance. It helped pull her into a seated position. She swung her legs over the side and eased down onto her feet. She was nothing short of amazed by how strong and steady she felt. Her thoughts flashed suddenly to the train about to slam into the truck she was in. A shock went through her whole being. How could she be here? What the hell was going on?! Just as suddenly, she remembered Gwendolyn had asked for her patience. She was trying hard to comply. Ally shook off her thoughts and looked at Gwendolyn, who was smiling.

"Please come with me, Allison." She requested.

The two women walked towards the blackness of the non-existent wall. As they neared, a door appeared. They stepped through it. Ally used her thin folded arms in a feeble attempt to hide her nakedness.

They walked silently down a long hallway with the same dim light as the room they had just exited. Gwendolyn came to a stop and used her hand to gesture to the left. Again, a door appeared out of nowhere. Ally followed closely behind her guide. They entered yet another dimly lit empty room, with one exception. Suspended in mid-air in the center of the room was a shiny silver jumpsuit like Gwendolyn was wearing.

"I hope that's for me." Ally said shyly, quite aware of her naked body.

"It is, go ahead." Gwendolyn nodded towards the sleek garment.

The suit fit perfectly as if it were tailor-made just for her because it was.

Soon they found their way to another room devoid of walls. This one had cafeteria-style tables in straight, neat rows. Some of the tables were occupied. Scattered about the room, random people looked happy, and content eating meals served on rectangular trays.

Gwendolyn invited Ally to sit opposite herself at one of the sterile tables. Ally lowered herself into a seated position on the long bench. Her patience waned. She folded her hands in front of her and let them rest on the table. She locked her gaze on the beauty across from her, searching her face for any sign of what she wasn't sure.

Ally's mind was bursting with questions. It took everything she had to keep herself from lunging over the table at Gwendolyn and shaking her violently until she purged out every last answer.

"Why am I here? Is this heaven? Hell? Why am I unscathed after being dismembered in a fatal train wreck? How did I get here???"

Gwendolyn recognized Ally's ever-increasing anxiousness. She had seen it in others many times before. She reached out and patted Ally's tightly clenched fists.

" Allison," cooed Gwendolyn. "I understand how you are feeling. But I need to ask you again to be patient and relax." Ally sat frozen, hoping for much more. Gwendolyn continued.

"I will try and explain your new situation as clearly as possible. But there is a lot to cover. Some of the information will seem unbelievable. I'm asking you just to have faith that I am telling you the truth. Soon all the information will come together and make sense. Not long from now, it will all be perfectly normal for you."

The young newcomer let her shoulders relax a bit. She felt herself start to trust Gwendolyn, though she wasn't sure why. Gwendolyn sat up straight and laced her long fingers together in front of her. An enthusiastic, bright, and perfect smile practically swallowed her entire face. It made Ally think of those girls on game shows that gracefully wave their perfect hands over fabulous prizes and flip oversized tags to reveal actual retail prices. The normalcy of the thought gave her comfort and prompted an amused grin.

Gwendolyn's face turned suddenly sober. She would be as concise as possible. She wanted to be compassionate without mincing words. She focused on Ally and began to speak.

"Allison, you may or may not remember that your body died in a horrible accident."

" I remember." Ally replied. Her tone made clear to Gwendolyn that details were unwelcome.

Gwendolyn nodded in understanding. "Our Captain here on Rom was aware of your fate long before it happened. You had been selected to join this ship for reasons you will soon understand." Gwendolyn was pleased to notice Ally was remaining calm and patient. Most previous trainees had interrupted by now.

" Your soul was stored in what I can only describe as a kind of limbo chamber. Meanwhile, your new body was being duplicated, using your own organic matter's DNA."

Ally's eyes widened, and her eyebrows arched. She remained silent and attentive as Gwendolyn continued.

"It was duplicated carefully. We have the technology, skills, and necessary tools to replicate any life form, down to the smallest detail. Your body looks like it did before, but nothing is original, except for your soul." Gwendolyn paused. She thought for sure Ally would want to interject. She didn't. She remained silent with a look of concern. So, she continued.

"The soul is the individual. It alone makes us who we are. Our bodies are merely its vehicle. You have a new vehicle, Ally. It's as simple as that. Of course, you don't think of it as possible because in the world you are from, it's not. Rom's creator has been in existence far longer than your mind can currently comprehend. We are currently parked outside of time as you know it. Dimensionally it is not comprehensible to describe except by equations, and then most human minds still can barely grasp a summary of it. Needless to say. We are from your future, or a future timeline similar to the one you are from."

Gwendolyn paused and searched Ally's face. She thought she saw signs of genuine effort to understand.

"Please rest assured it will all come together soon and feel quite normal, natural." With that, she believed she had shared enough for now.

Ally shifted her attention from Gwendolyn to the hands spread on the table in front of her. Were they her hands? Well, Yes and No. She studied them carefully. First, she noticed the absence of her coveted jade ring. She remembered when her dad gave it to her as a high school graduation gift to wear at the ceremony. It had perfectly matched her eyes and her cap and gown. A tear came to her eye as she remembered how excited he was to watch her slip it on her trembling finger. She wondered where it was now.

Ally continued her inspection. Gwendolyn had said that even the most minor details could be duplicated, but hers weren't. Her hands were devoid of hair, fingerprints, and blemishes. They were flawless. Maybe they just decided to make a few improvements? She didn't mind, not at all.

Ally's attention was once again directed to Gwendolyn. She was anxiously waiting to hear Ally's thoughts.

Ally spoke, but what she said caught her off guard.

"I need a mirror!" Ally demanded with a sense of urgency.

Gwendolyn smiled and told Ally to take her arms off the table. Ally would have found a mirror rising out of a table-top to be truly miraculous in any other place or time. But by no means did she consider it normal, not yet anyway. It slowly revealed her new yet familiar image as it continued to ascend. Again, she began a careful study. As on her hands, her face had no hair, lines, or blemishes. Even the tiny scar on her chin was gone. She had tripped over the family cat in the kitchen on the way to put her dinner dish in the sink. The image in her mind of George, the obese orange tabby, made her go misty and yet produce a semi-silent chuckle accompanied by a wide grin. After turning her head from side to side a few times, she was happy with her improved image. The mirror descended, and her view was once again Gwendolyn.

Gwendolyn's expression was begging for Ally's opinion.

" You people sure know how to work an airbrush." Ally teased.

Gwendolyn smiled and winked. Then quickly took on a se-riousness. Once again, Gwendolyn reached for Ally's hand.

She spoke in a friendly yet serious tone.

"Allison, in the days to come, you will be taking in a tremendous amount of new information. You will be noticing the vast differences and plenty of similarities between the people on Rom and Earth. You will be schooled about other planets as well. This will take a long time, as many other worlds are around us. Some near and some very far. We all have our uniqueness, but we all share one common bond. The one exception is Earth. It is understood that God is the ruler of all. Earth has many that deny him still. It has been long understood for us. God is in constant contact with us all. He will not directly contact the earth until they believe."

Ally felt relieved. Having always been a woman of faith, she was only human, a sinner. Conformation of God made her heart light, and she felt freedom from doubt, but she also was fearful for her native planet. What was to become of it?

"Thank you for telling me, Gwendolyn." She said with great sincerity.

Laqueesha and Tyrone finished their breakfasts. Laqueesha had enjoyed the oatmeal, fresh fruit, and buttered toast. Tyrone wasn't quite as impressed. He was more of an eggs and bacon kind of guy.

Gwendolyn turned her attention to the children. She noticed they were finished eating and asked Ally to excuse her momentarily.

Gwendolyn approached the young newcomers while smiling brightly. They both watched her as she spoke.

"Did you two enjoy your meals?" she asked eagerly.

"Very much, thank you!" Exclaimed Laqueesha.

"Tyrone?"

"It was ok, and I'm not into health food like Sis."

Gwendolyn had to laugh. His honesty was endearing. Laqueesha snorted and rolled her eyes, then scolded Tyrone.

"You know Tyrone, everything you eat is pure garbage! You're gonna eat yourself into an early grave!"

Gwendolyn smiled again and was happy to share some news. "Look, kids, things are different here on ROM as far as nutrition is concerned." She had their attention. "Earth food doesn't exist here. What you ate was food made from a highly nutritious compound. It may be manipulated to duplicate anything you like. You can request any kind of food from burgers to broccoli, and it will all be equally nutritious."

Laqueesha's jaw dropped. "Really?!"

Tyrone shot her a smug and triumphant look with a bonus middle finger.

"Still gonna eat that shitty rabbit food, tomorrow Sis?" He laughed.

"It's possible, asshole!" Laqueesha proclaimed stubbornly, knowing full well that pasties and sausage were in her future.

Gwendolyn gave an amused eye roll and a wide grin before returning to the table Ally was seated at. She placed an open palm on the young woman's back.

"Allison, would you come with me? I would like to introduce you to a couple of your fellow newcomers."

They walked up to the children, and Gwendolyn started the introduction.

"Tyrone, Laqueesha, this is Allison. She goes by Ally."

The three nodded and exchanged hellos.

Gwendolyn gestured to Ally, and they sat down with the kids.

"It's nice to meet you both. I'm glad to have company in the same situation." Ally added with sincerity.

"Allison, you must be starving!" Gwendolyn announced.

" I am!" She admitted.

Gwendolyn explained to Ally that today's pre-selection was oatmeal and fresh fruit. But that she could have her choice of anything else if that didn't interest her.

"This will be the first meal your new body will receive Ally, how exciting!" Gwendolyn told her.

Ally decided that the pre-selection sounded fine. She was just eager to cure the hunger pains. Tyrone decided against commenting on her choice. He figured she at least had a choice. Not his fault she blew the opportunity to have something good. Ally ate with enthusiasm; it was quickly consumed. She wiped her mouth and watched in amazement as the table consumed the tray.

"That will never cease to amaze me." She thought out loud.

"It will become completely normal to you in no time," Gwendolyn informed with a smile.

"Not a chance, Gwen," only this time her comment remained a silent thought.

Gwendolyn rose to her feet and announced that they would now embark on a tour.

"Today, you will be properly introduced to Rom, your new home. Please follow me."

They followed, feeling anxious but also excited. Their first stop down the dim hallway was what Gwendolyn said was a conference room. It was as simple as all the previous rooms. But this one had four chairs and what looked like a wall-sized screen directly in front of them. Gwendolyn asked them to

pick a chair and make themselves comfortable. They each settled in one of the sensible yet very comfortable chairs. Laqueesha performed a few butt bounces and settled back.

The screen came to life, literally. A man stood in front
of what they all assumed was ROM outside. It was different
then the earth's outside. The sky was a light purple, and the
trees were unfamiliar yet were definitely trees. There wasn't
any recognizable foliage. It was almost surreal. Ally thought
to herself, one day soon, I will find it all perfectly normal. The
thought amused her, and she felt a small smile invade her lips.

"Welcome, Allison, Laqueesha, Tyrone." His head nodded
in the direction of each of his welcomees as he stated their
names.

"I'm James. I've been on ROM for the past 45 years. I am
originally from Earth."

He appeared to be in his early to mid-60s, slightly stocky
with dark hair combed straight back. He paced back and
forth as he spoke. His hands pressed together by his finger-
tips.

"I want you all to understand that I know exactly what it's
like to wake up in a new world." He paused and scanned their
faces.

"I'm here to help you. Today I will be giving you what we
call the transition tour." He resumed his pacing.

"You will tour some of our nature as well as some of our
public structures, but most importantly, Gwendoline and I
will answer any questions you have."

He nodded in acknowledgment to Gwendoline. She
smiled and returned the nod. Gwendolyn stood from her
chair Ann faced them.

"Hopefully by the end of today, you will have a sense of normalcy. Please keep an open mind and it positive attitude. Today is the first day of the rest of your new life!" She winked at them; and joined James in front of the live background. James continued.

"On that note, expect to be amazed and delighted!"

Gwendolyn waved them forward. The seated trio exchanged wide-eyed glances.

" Let's get started!" she gushed with enthusiasm.

Laqueesha whispered to Tyrone. "I'm kind of freaking, but excited too!"

He nodded. " Same here!"

They stepped through the screen which was actually an opening to the outside of the facility. The same sun that shines on earth was high in the purple sky of Rom that morning. The three newbies stood silently in awe of their new planet's beauty. A voice broke the silence.

"As you can see, the landscape is similar to that of earth's, and yet quite different. There is no vegetation here that can also be found on earth." James stated.

Then bent down to pick a flower, one they had never seen before. He handed it to Ally, she instinctually brought it to her nose. She breathed in and closed her eyes. "Mmmm" She cooed.

James went on. "As on earth, there are different regions, each containing different climates, vegetation and landscapes. And like earth, we breathe oxygen and consume food and water."

As he walked forward, they all followed. He continued speaking as he strolled. "There are many other planets in many galaxies around us. Some near some quite far. Most contain some form of life. Many in human form, but far from all. Some breathe oxygen while others breathe different elements. Some don't need water, while others don't consume food. You will have many opportunities to learn about these places throughout your lifetime here. He stopped and turned to face them "but there is one thing all planets have in common. God."

They walked and listened and asked questions. They learned that after completing Transition, they would each be assigned a home and occupation. They were all pleased to hear it, especially Tyrone. He hoped they were looking for basketball players. They walked on. They studied plants, observed wildlife, and even toured an available home. The day was warm, and the air smelled of fresh flowers, (of some sort).

Half of the day had passed before Tyrone made a statement. "I'm hungry," he said. Laqueesha agreed.

James replied with a wide grin "well, I guess this would be a good time to introduce you to ROMs answer to the restaurant."

They walked up to and entered a building called sustenance. All eating establishments on ROM we're called "Sustenance." They were fueling stations for the body. On earth, they were more like a source of entertainment. Here they were merely a place to eat if you weren't at or near your home. After walking through the front sliding glass door, they followed James to an elevator, where he began to scan the menu of buttons. His finger stopped on the one that was labeled earth and pushed it.

Ally remarked, "You seem to have been here before."

James informed her that all sustenance stations were the same. And that he had been in many of them, but he had never been to this particular building. The doors parted and they filed in and turned around. The door closed. Then almost immediately, they opened back up. They hadn't felt any movement or experienced that weird whoosh in your stomach that happens when an elevator on earth stops.

James stepped out first." Here we are."

They didn't even ask, just decided to go with the flow. He led them around a corner and through an open archway. The room was started with people sitting and eating around circular tables. James pressed another button. This one was on a wall panel labeled with numbers he pressed the number 5. As magically as everything else on ROM, a table rose out of the floor surrounded by five chairs. They all chose a seat. In front of each of them, the table displayed a menu.

James explained. "Everyone read the selections. Then when you know what you want, touch your choice. That's all there is to it."

Laqueesha remembered what Gwendoline had told them about the earth food all being recreated from some substance and that it was all equal in nutrition.

She thought to herself, "no more fuckin' salads for me!"

She had a sly smile on her face as she pressed her finger on the fried chicken and mashed potatoes with gravy selection. Tyrone enthusiastically chose the double cheeseburger and fries. Ally thought as she scanned the menu. Suddenly she stiffened and looked wide-eyed at James.

"Is this food made out of the same organic shit as me?!"

He wasn't expecting that one. He looked at Gwendolyn as if to say will you take this one?

Gwendoline smiled at Ally and explained, "Allison, let me put it simply. You're alive. Your food isn't."

"So, yes?" Ally demanded.

Gwendolyn confirmed. "Yes, but in a completely different form sweetie."

"Don't tell me, let me guess... In no time at all, I'll find it completely normal." Ally droned in a condescending tone.

Tyrone laughed aloud, it made Laqueesha giggle into the back of her hand. Ally pushed her finger to the word Taco salad.

Laqueesha asked James if Tyrone And herself were also made from what Ally was made from.

"No Laqueesha, you and your brother arrived in your earthly bodies and remain in them. Allison, not unlike myself, arrived here as only souls. Our bodies died on Earth. ROM constructed new bodies for our souls to reside in until our next lives." He stated simply.

Laqueesha stared at James in amazement. "Don't worry Laqueesha, it will all seem perfectly normal soon!" Ally teased.

Gwendolyn had to smile and shake her head. They ate their meals in silence, but with enthusiasm.

That evening Gwendolyn and James agreed to meet for a cocktail and discuss the day's events and progress. James was already sipping on a beverage, not unlike earthly bourbon. Gwendolyn greeted him and sat heavily into the comfortable chair. "I'm beat" she blurted as she pressed the word wine on the table before her.

James, after a generous sip, asked her how she thought

things went today. Gwendoline half-emptied her glass before she answered. "I think it went as well as any other transition day." She downed the rest of the wine and pressed the 'order same' selection.

"I must say though, this is one of my favorite groups, to date anyway. They have a sort of offbeat humor to them" James agreed.

With that, Gwendolyn picked up her wine glass and made short work of it.

The Universe has unified to save the earth from its 2082 extinction. A plan was set in motion in 1960. Key people have been selected and brought to ROM since it was implemented. People with many different skills sets and strengths. Some were in current important positions and some were brought in before their earthly destinies were fulfilled. People such as Allison who had her earthly existence continued would have become a Supreme Court justice. Had Laqueesha and Tyrone remained on earth, they would have become the most renowned pair of biochemists of their century. This army was taking shape to begin the process of saving the earth from its self-destructive, naive, and godless self.

Gwendolyn rose from her seat. "it's been a long day; I think I'll turn in early."

She walked to the back of her chair and pushed it under the table. Then preceded for the door that would appear before her.

James called out from behind her. "Goodnight, Gwen" he teased and grinned, knowing she didn't like when people shortened her name.

She stopped and looked back at him. "Goodnight to you too, Mr. Hoffa." Then disappeared into the darkness.

26

Saved In Time

27

Cindy stared up at the slivers of blue sky beyond the branches of the snow-covered Douglas fir trees. Her gloved hands rested gently around the branch protruding from her belly. She blinked periodically to keep her eyeballs from freezing. At least that's what she thought. She had never been so cold in her life. She didn't think she could move, even if it were possible.

She didn't know how long it had been since Danny went for help. 5 minutes? Two hours? All she knew was that time seemed to stand still, locking her misery in place. Cindy felt herself fading out of consciousness. It felt good. She slipped into what may or may not have been a dream.

Cindy walked through the front door. It didn't look like her house, but somehow, she knew she was home. Navigating the rooms came naturally, even though she had never seen them before. She found her mom sitting at the dining room table. She was clutching a black coffee cup in one hand and thumbing through a tabloid with the other.

"Hi mom, I'm home!" she chimed excitedly.

Her mother looked up slowly from the magazine. "Where is Cindy?" She asked, obviously puzzled.

"Ha-ha, mom, you're hilarious."

Her mother didn't respond. She only licked her finger and turned to the next page. Cindy stood and stared at her for a moment, not understanding the question. Suddenly her father entered the room through the sliding glass door to the left of the table. He walked over to her mom, leaned down, and kissed the top of her head.

"Hello Lori, I've missed you."

Lori didn't seem to know he was there and just continued reading. Cindy was overwhelmed to see him. "Daddy?"

He looked up at her and smiled. He said only one thing.

"Come home, your mother needs you."

Cindy's eyes snapped open, instantly reminding her of her reality. She came out of the dream with a sense of hope. Her father's words had given her a reason to believe there may be a way through this impossible situation. She had to stay patient, strong, and pray.

The rescue pod appeared on the mountain, and it hovered weightlessly over the undisturbed white powdery snow. James instructed his crew. "We need to work quickly; we don't want to be detected."

Henry, Ally, and Gwendolyn nodded in agreement.

"Ally, we will extract you from the pod first. You will be her support system. Keep her calm and reassured that she will be fine."

Ally stood and walked to the transport chamber with solid confidence.

She informed them with a self-assured voice. "I'm ready to go!"

Henry navigated the Control Board skillfully. Ally faded

from their sight. The remaining crew sprang into action. The mission was in motion.

Ally lay a soft open palm on Cindy's forehead. Feeling the comforting warmth of the welcome touch, she filled with a glorious sense of relief. She opened her eyes and smiled at the lovely face above her own.

"Hello Cindy, I'm Ally. My friends and I are here to help you."

Cindy's voice was soft and yet raspy from the cold. "Did Danny find you? Is he here?"

Before she could answer, Gwendolyn's footsteps crunched loudly through the snow and brittle twigs. She approached and stopped. She stood beside the kneeling Ally. She looked down at Cindy.

"Hello, young lady, we're going to take care of you. Try and relax the best you can. Alison will be by your side the whole time."

Her smile was warm and sincere as she turned and took several steps back. She paused momentarily and spoke into a small device strapped to her wrist.

"James, we're going to need the fluoroscope."

Gwendolyn walked back to Ally and Cindy. They waited. Soon James appeared with something that Cindy thought was a kind of drone. As James approached, the fluoroscope hovered and followed behind him. He stopped and stood at Cindy's feet. He had a large pouch slung over his shoulder. Cindy watched him carefully. She offered him a small smile. He reciprocated and threw in a wink for reassurance.

James reached in the pouch and withdrew a small, zippered case, which he then handed to Gwendolyn. She tugged at the zipper, and the case folded open. She screwed a long needle onto the syringe and filled it with the liquid from a little bottle. She lifted the concoction and tapped the side of the glass.

Cindy's eyes grew unnaturally wide at the sight of the extreme length of the needle. Ally patted her on the shoulder in reassurance.

Gwendolyn explained. "Please don't be alarmed. We had to plan on penetrating through all of your clothing layers. Very little of the actual needle will penetrate your thigh."

Cindy's anxiety eased a bit. Gwendolyn injected the liquid into Cindy's flesh.

"Cindy, you should be more comfortable momentarily."

She put the empty injection back into the case and zipped it up. She handed it to James and began to explain. "This shot will make your body warm up to a normal temperature. In addition, it will ease your pain and help you relax. Soon after, you will fall into a profound sleep. You will wake up warm and safe, far from this mountain."

Cindy felt the warmth slowly engulf her being. It was the most amazing feeling she had ever experienced. The pain was long forgotten. She drifted away into the sleep of a lifetime.

The crew worked swiftly and efficiently. The fluoroscope confirmed what they had initially suspected. Cindy's lower body would not survive.

They worked harmoniously as they carefully separated Cindy's upper and lower body. The technology on ROM made this a semisimple and quick procedure. The work was flawless. Cindy would remain in a coma for several weeks. She would wake when the reconstruction of her body was complete.

Cindy woke slowly out of her deep long sleep. She found it difficult to open her eyes at first. It was as if they had been glued shut. She rubbed at them with her fists until her lids broke free. The little light in the room assaulted them regardless of its weakness. Before she could get them focused, she heard a voice.

"Ally?" she croaked, her throat achy and dry.

"Yes, it's me, Ally. I brought you a drink of water".

Cindy struggled to sit up. Ally reached around her back and helped her into an upright position.

"Where am I?" she asked in a confused tone.

"You're safe in our Infirmary; please take a sip." She said as she offered the water.

Cindy cupped her hands around the plastic cup and drank greedily.

"Whoa, whoa, slowly at first!"

She offered the cup back to Ally and let out an exhausted gasp.

"Thanks, I was so thirsty." She said through a windy exhale.

It took a few minutes for Cindy's memory to fully recover. A startled look came over her face. Her hands suddenly grasped at her stomach. She felt for the branch that had been there the last time she looked. It was gone! Her mouth gaped open in disbelief.

"I'm healed, but how?!"

Ally had prepared in advance for the question.

"You've been here for quite some time now, Cindy. Our medicine is quite advanced, compared to your 1980s techniques."

Cindy was skeptical. She understood she wasn't the

brightest girl in the world, but she also knew she wasn't an idiot. This was impossible. She should be dead, or at the very least severely maimed. This was a miracle, nothing less.

Ally could see Cindy's frustration and skepticism.

"Cindy, everything will be explained in time. All your questions will be fully answered."

Gwendolyn suddenly popped into Ally's mind. How many times did Gwendolyn assure her that soon all of this would seem quite normal? She thought about how much she had doubted it. Now, it turns out that the bitch was right. The thought made her smile and shake her head.

Ally held up a silver jumpsuit in front of Cindy. She asked if she would like help putting it on. Cindy reached for the garment and looked it over carefully. "No, I think I can manage," Cindy said, almost begrudgingly.

She poked both of her legs through the holes of the jumpsuit and slid to the floor. She zipped up the front and smoothed her hands down her sides. It was a perfect fit.

Ally led Cindy out of the dimly lit room into an equally dim hallway. Ally paused. A door appeared. With a nod of her head, Ally gestured toward a table that seated several people. It was time for lunch and some introductions.

2 8

God Knows Your Heart

Who is the United States?

When is it in the best interest of the United States to violate the rights of the people in the best interest of the United States?

That sounds absurd. If it is in the best interest of the American people, then of course, in a normal situation America, the United States of America, and its people would choose what is best for the people.

We the people of the United States, are the United States of America. Our representatives are selected by consent. They serve the people by the will of the people. Who have elected these folks to positions within the government by conducting elections throughout our country. Those who win the trust of the majority of their constituents represent them for a set period of time.

The consent of the governed is the key. Consent gives power, and then only for a period of time. There is a problem when consent is not given. That makes sense to the average person. Who doesn't understand the issues that arise when something is taken without consent?

If I take something from you without your permission, it is theft. You understand that. Our ancestors have understood that this is about giving permission. You must give permission to use or take your property, or your person. Without consent, you are a victim of a criminal violation.

You have a legitimate right to compensation. You have a right to redress your grievance. You have had these rights in some form since before our nation's founding. This is not a new concept. I'm not teaching you something you may not be aware of.

Since the 18th century, and I am not talking in the year of our Lord AD. I'm talking before Christ, the king of Babylon, hammered out a written code of law. These laws were written in stone by King Hammurabi, and judges were appointed to enforce them.

Indeed, there were laws and ordinances before then. They just have not survived through to our day. Still, that gives us as a people an adequate background and basis for understanding good, evil, right, wrong. Almost four thousand years worth of understanding and documentation exists.

Robbery, rape, fraud, vandalism, and of course, murder have been extensively discussed, practiced, and tried. From these tests of time, we know what to do when someone has violated these ordinances that name the various crimes.

When your rights as a man under such laws are removed without due process of law. When they are removed without the conviction of a court, when judges refuse to hear the case against the one who has taken your property, this is also a crime. We have thousands of years worth of case history documenting this.

No rational man would give his right to representation up willingly. Tricking and subverting his will with lies is fraudulent. There is no right to keep what you have stolen. Just because power holds justice out of reach from those who know that fraud has been committed does not give credence to any argument that the perpetrators have to holding on to the property, wealth, and titles gained through deceit. The complicit are criminals. They are accessories and guilty as well of theft. The theft of the content of the governed is terrible and terrifying. It is just as, if not more so, as awful as the commission of rape or murder.

When election fraud has taken place at all levels of society, just this fact is enough to break the constructs of society's infrastructure. When you add to it massive theft of the people's wealth by those who have stolen their positions. Who pretend to represent the people. This compounds the problem. If these official malefactors have no fear of justice.

No sheriff comes to arrest or detain them.

No Attorney General holds them accountable.

No judge applies justice.

This leaves the people with little recourse. The populace will fall back on their inalienable rights. Those rights are given to them by God. You suppose that our state is secular. This is a mistaken assumption.

Our country is founded on deep spiritual beliefs. It is recognized in all the founding materials left us by our forefathers. Which faith or religion that is followed is immaterial. The point is our legal system is built on these precepts.

That the rights are given to us by God.

Written law, from the beginning, insists on at least this one point as a basis. Hammurabi himself insisted his original written laws were given to him by God. Moses received the commandments from God. Our inalienable rights, the ones we have fought for over centuries, have been given to us by God

"to which the laws of nature and of Nature's God entitle them, a decent respect."

Our Bill of Rights is a list of rights given to us by the almighty God. With our first right not forming a secular government but instead establishing our right to worship. Our right to practice our religion.

There is no way to carefully craft evil little laws around that statement as the first right of all Americans and further the rights of all men worldwide. These are rights bestowed on man by God, and that is not just American men. That is men, women, and children worldwide.

The freedom of religion
The freedom of speech
The freedom of the press
The freedom of assembly
The right to redress your grievances

These rights are all bestowed on us by God. We the people are merely caretakers of them. These rights come with extraordinary obligations. The entire world looks to the United States of America to hold these rights above and out of reach of tampering by bitter, evil, little men that lack character and conviction to do the right thing in the face of opportunity calling to them from Pinocchio's Pleasure Island. Carlo Collodi's tale of the adventures of our favorite wooden toy calls out to us here now in his future as a warning more than just a delightful tale for kids. Do the right thing, even if it is hard.

Tearing down the basic building blocks of our society is not based on any godly principle. It is an atheistic attack on the fabric of our culture. When the rule of law is flaunted in our legislative houses across our nation. The legislators, senators, judges, and executives appear to be oblivious that the eyes of God look at their actions. They laugh at the outrages committed while they fill their purses from the taxpayer's treasures.

Which rights do you willingly give to evil people?

Just the unimportant ones?

Which one is unimportant?

How many political prisoners are allowable?

How many children sold into slavery is acceptable?

Is only a handful of child brides slipping through our fingers, alright?

Bad news is tearing down our legal processes and building them back better. Turning our society better, but better for whom? This is a trick. It is a trick by our adversary to enslave the entire world. It inhibits all rights given to us by God, building back better into a world encompassed in slavery where only the rich and powerful can expect liberty or happiness.

Very few can expect the opportunity to pursue happiness in the coming dystopian future. This place where there is no separation of industry from the government. It is your obligation and duty as Americans to disrupt these events. Inhibiting their final execution is the duty of everyone. It is the obligation of Nobody in particular, and all of us entirely. We have this obligation because we have enjoyed the rights bestowed on us by God.

These things are not easy, and they will not stay swept under the rug. They are hard, pointy with sharp horns. The stag won't remain hidden in the brush; he must come out. It is instinctual. Don't believe for a moment that he is not a formidable opponent.

We are in for the fight of our lives. The future and the past meet. They never separate. God sees it all, and God knows your heart.

Lightning Source UK Ltd.
Milton Keynes UK
UKHW020640291221
396330UK00011B/741